TAKING DOWN THE MOON
LISA MUIR

67 Press
Winston Salem, North Carolina

This book is a work of fiction. Names, characters, places and incidents either are a product of the author's imagination or are used fictitiously. Any resemblance to actual events or locales or persons living or dead is entirely coincidental.

TAKING DOWN THE MOON
Copyright © Lisa Muir 2016

Vanilla Tuna was previously published in *Affinity: an Anthology* published by 67 Press.

Cover Art and Design by Matt Ankerson.
Cover Layout by Bradley Powell

ISBN 978-0-9966616-1-4

Manufactured in the United States

For anyone who ever gave me any kind of support or encouragement.

And Ken, who gives me nothing but.

TABLE OF CONTENTS

TAKING DOWN THE MOON

THE LOUCHE WATERMELON QUEEN

She needed someone to die to stop eating. Someone whose sudden absence would so depress her—just temporarily—making sustenance repugnant. That way she'd lose a load of weight quickly and then, once recovered from the terrible loss, be that much ahead in the weight loss project. It didn't even have to be someone that close—she wasn't cruel—but then again without a deep emotional connection she'd likely go back to overeating soon after the funeral. She wanted to be thin for the cruise—former 1988 Watermelon Queen of Fair Bluff, Tennessee, and all. It was Ron's fault anyway, this feeling of inadequacy. If he hadn't called her corpulent—and then *laughed* when she ran to the dictionary—she wouldn't be wishing for death. But a tragedy would be best at this point.

She sharpened her knife. Not a real one, but the resurrected oyster knife of Zora Neale Hurston, the carver of well-placed words. But she wasn't very good at effecting a real death with its subsequent funereal consequences. Her sister was a prime candidate, but they had recently made up. Her brother-in-law needed wiping out daily, but ... her sister. Neighbors weren't dear enough and the annoying check-out woman at ShopWorld was too distant. So out of the blue in revenge for the "corpulent" comment, she told her husband she had never married him for love, that her passion had been his younger brother (long dead), and marrying Ron had been the only way to stay close. It wasn't true, but a risk was needed. Her words would wound her husband deeply, which would make her sad. Would he fight for her? She would agonize over what she had done. She wept.

She was on her way.

YOU CAN'T COLLECT TIME

Lanie knew the high probability of meeting an eligible man in the grocery for she read *O Magazine* and *Cosmo* and *New Living*. In addition, she was up on Oprah, Dr. Phil, and Dr. Oz, catching reruns in the early evening when necessary. It happened just as Lanie knew it would—not imagined but *knew* it would—for the moment's arrival had long left the realm of fantasy in her mind and organized itself into a plan. She had considered the moment in the finest of detail and here it was.

She grocery shopped nearly every day, considering it European, a habit her friend Bella considered wasteful. "Shop once a week and save time and gas," Bella scoffed. But how did one meet a man that way?

The register clerk rang up Lanie's purchases and then bagged them. Lanie paid the young woman in slow motion, wondering what she would see when she turned toward the Customer Service area directly to her right. Would he be standing there? He had to be. He had gazed at her multiple times that evening, with longing she felt, while she had walked the aisles choosing dinner purchases. They had smiled politely as their encounters became frequent, she walking up an aisle, he walking down. Or maybe it was the other way around, he walking up and she walking down. No one gave directions in the grocery. No one gave her directions at all anymore. She and this attractive man could give one another direction, help each other through life.

In just a moment she would be through with her transaction and be able to walk straight toward him, he who would be waiting for her, leaning languidly against the wall near Customer Service. She chuckled at the new meaning of Customer *Service*.

But with the confusion of her heavy celery lolling from one side of the bag's rim to the other, threatening to topple the entire thing and its contents, she riveted her attention to the green stalks, righting them uselessly just before they flopped out of the bag completely, spilling the entire contents across the clerk's conveyor belt. She hadn't meant to look so frantic, and when she was finally able to glance at the wall to her right, she saw no one—which was not part of the plan.

The clerk captured the items, rebagging them, and tensely Lanie scooped up the sack, her left arm around the brown paper, squeezing it as though it were a plump, indignant baby. But in attempting to use her right hand to smooth the sides of her jacket, now gathered in unflattering bunches, she obscured her view as she hefted her purchases in front of her face. A skein of her long hair caught on the rim of the bag and then dropped into her mouth. She gagged. Why hadn't she brought her nifty and environmentally pleasing *Let's Recycle!* cloth tote with handles?

Yet, when she lowered the sack and pulled the wet hair out of her mouth, there he was walking right toward her, just like in the movies. Where had he been? He made an arc, curving himself into a space beside her which was neither threatening nor strange. And he was direct but polite, no stammering or awkwardness in his greeting.

"I've seen you here before," he smiled, completely forgetting the oval carton of ice cream sitting at the top of his own purchases.

.   .   .

Lanie and Bella had had a conversation about their individual attraction to men only once, Bella being long married and not understanding the dating selection process here at fifty-five years old. The discussion had not begun with men but with political leaders, turning to Yassar Arafat, dead for years, whom Bella had then called one of the most unattractive men on earth.

"I always thought he was kind of good looking," confessed Lanie.

Had Bella been in control of the vehicle rather than Lanie, her surprise would have caused her to drive into a ditch.

"Good looking? Heavens, who thinks Arafat was *good looking?*"

"Maybe not good looking, but sort of cute in that droopy kind of way."

"Good God, even if I did know single men to match you up with, I wouldn't do so now. How could I pick someone out for you if it's Arafat you've wanted all along?"

"I don't *want* Arafat, but that droopy look just works for me."

"Most people would call that a hangdog look and consider it rather undesirable."

"I am not most people," said Lanie, unfazed by Bella's assessment. "So who's cute to you? George Clooney? I like him."

"Somewhat too slick for me."

"Yes, but good looking?"

"Well, he reminds me of that guy in *Pretty Woman*, Richard Gere. They're both too put together."

5

"Y-e-s, but good looking?"

"Too fashioned for my taste."

"You mean their clothes?"

"No, I mean they come across as unreal, as creations, that slicked down hair, the constant perfect lines, never seeming anything but calm and collected on the entertainment shows."

"Well, maybe they are and that's what's so desirable about them," Lanie rationalized.

"Maybe … to others. I did like one guy in a movie about drug wars Steve and I saw recently. I can't remember the name though."

"I've never seen a drug movie. So how about Liam Neeson?"

"He's rather hulking."

"I have to admit I don't think The Hulk was good looking either," answered Lanie, her mind reverting to the late seventies show.

"You're completely missing the point."

"I am?"

"I don't mean the green guy, Lou Ferrigno. I mean he's rather hulking in size. Even his head is big."

Lanie snorted.

"But don't get me wrong. He's a terrific actor. I loved him in *Les Miserables* and *Kinsey* too."

Lanie stared straight ahead at the road.

"You should check out that drug movie," Bella insisted.

"I don't watch drug movies."

· · ·

Lanie and the man each held their groceries which mercifully gave them something to do with their hands. She figured later he could carry her bag to her car, one in each strong arm, and wondered whether in disclosing their purchases to one other, they would discover they could form a romantic meal together.

He asked her to the café at the end of the plaza. "That's safe, isn't it?"

She calmly admitted it was, though her heart raced beneath the bag she now clutched.

As they walked the length of the shopping plaza they passed the movie rental place where Lanie bought cheap DVD versions of old films she'd already seen rather than renting new ones. "Rent something *current*," Bella had groused once, but Lanie would only watch movies with happy endings she could count on. She and this man could always talk old movies if the conversation ran dry. As they walked Lanie recalled a title or two just in case.

She found out his name was Eric, the same as her older brother, which gave her a comfortable feeling. A decade older, her brother had been protective of her as a child. Both men had saucer eyes and this new Eric's hair had rarely seen a comb yet somehow wasn't limp.

Over black coffee Lanie explained to this new Eric that she was a painter, not a very good one, but able to make a living. He seemed impressed, especially coming from the business world. She told him about her small but cozy house and the many birds she kept for company. Her house could be quite noisy she admitted, and yet the room's light affected the birds' feathers and could turn dull colors into shimmering hues, influencing the brush strokes on her palette. Moreover, the birds' chatter affected her spirit in wonderful ways.

"One of my birds makes it into each of my paintings, though I'm never sure which one or where when I start. I do mostly landscapes, so to incorporate a bird isn't that difficult. It's kind of my signature and I hear that some people even look for the bird when my work hangs at a show. That's how I make my living, though I don't attend the shows much."

She drank in the details of Eric's globe-trotting, which revealed his curiosity rather than privilege. He had traveled a great deal but she had not. She had grown up in the area, graduating from the local university, then chose to stay put. Little had changed since. If she went out to eat, which she found difficult to do as a single woman, she stuck with the same establishments where she had eaten thirty years ago as a college student. Of the newer restaurants in town she knew nothing. She sometimes roamed the downtown area, for inspiration she told herself, recalling businesses where she had worked as a college student, though much had changed and no one she knew worked there anymore. For two pleasant years in college she had been employed at a card shop, located conveniently on a corner, which had now turned into a small take-out sandwich restaurant. Sometimes she would stand in the middle of the establishment's tables, even while students ate, remembering former Hallmark displays she had tidied. She never ordered a sandwich. The employees, all in their twenties, saw her as a weird but harmless woman who hovered briefly and then disappeared.

In her home her furniture consisted of the same stuff she had dragged from her family home to her first college apartment and then to subsequently larger apartments in the same town—a checked chair from her grandmother, the tan plaid sofa from her mother's house, a cousin's old double bed. If asked she would claim the pieces were antiques, but their tattered appearance spoke otherwise. Though she had moved away from the student ghetto she'd occupied as an undergraduate, at fifty-five years old she still lived in the equivalent of a college dump.

Eric asked about her friends and she countered with the fact that she lived in a lovely neighborhood—without revealing that she knew none of her neighbors beyond a wave of recognition from the driver's seat on her way to and from running an errand. Lanie contended she wanted to join social and civic groups, even naming them—The River Rats, who cleaned up the local waterways, Bare Nutrition, which advocated the growing of organic foods, and Rainbow Perspective, a group of local artists—but she only *talked* about doing so, never seeking the groups out, even in the phonebook. She would wander downtown to the university library, but only to grieve over a previous college rental house which had once sat where the blacktop parking lot now spanned. She dressed peculiarly, appearing out of date in some vague way, yet she had been saved by the recent retro craze, never having given away any of her clothes over the past decades. What would have been discarded by most years ago still hung neatly in the closets of her two bedrooms.

Of course she revealed little of this analysis to Eric in the coffee shop. Instead, she watched his long fingers curl around the mug, his eyes trained on her with obvious interest. She felt new and different. He was tall, thin, and serious. He had a solid position in the banking world. Prior to this moment she had sometimes awakened in the morning vowing to make a small decision just to feel she was moving forward at some point in the day. The thrill she felt at Eric's presence, his arm so close to her own on the glass tabletop, simultaneously made her realize her stasis.

Before each of them knew it an hour had passed, and the dregs of their coffee had begun to dry at the bottom of each mug.

"May I see you again?" he had asked with such gallantry. He might as well have bent down on one knee, but of course he did nothing so ridiculous. They made a date: he would come for dinner. They could eat on her porch, he suggested. She could lock the front door. He promised to be no threat. Lanie laughed, but logically considered her options.

Lanie picked up her bag of groceries, long forgotten at her feet, and Eric did the same. There would be no kiss—it was far too early—but the handshake they attempted turned into an awkward hug, especially given that each clutched a group of fairly unbalanced food products. Lanie's stalks of celery felt hard and phallic against her chest, but a sense of warmth emanated from Eric, something she hadn't experienced in years. And then suddenly the top of Eric's vanilla ice cream popped off its container, spewing melted white cream onto his arm.

"I forgot I'd bought frozen stuff," he faltered for the first time that evening as he leaned back to reach for the napkin holder standing in the middle of the table where the two had abandoned their coffee mugs. "I'll take care of this," he suggested with embarrassment. "I'll see you soon."

Lanie's sense of satisfaction was deep and profound.

.   .   .

He hadn't realized the birds would be flying freely in the house, cockatiels and lovebirds mostly and some sort of blue bird he couldn't identify. Maybe two or three of those blue birds. He also hadn't anticipated the clocks—multiple clocks, clocks nearly everywhere he looked. Lanie had not kept him on the porch, and right now they were in the house as much as he had expected to be out, for the screen doors had to be securely fastened to avoid the birds' escape.

"They love me but they're so inquisitive," explained Lanie. "Sometimes I put the cages outside so they can interact with the wild birds. I'm not sure if that's cruel or not because in some sense they must know how imprisoned they are. That's why I let them fly free here in the house."

"But isn't there, um—"

"Bird shit everywhere?" finished Lanie.

"Yeah."

"Yes, but I just clean it up. Comes with territory. Notice I've got no curtains hanging? Which is why I keep the birds out of my own bedroom because there I do have curtains, of course. Plus, the birds aren't always out. They fly back into their cages too. They feel warm and safe there."

"Except this one." Lanie pointed to a male cockatiel sitting atop a lampshade, its red crest standing straight up, the bird alert to the stranger's presence. "That's Jefferson and he makes every attempt he can to get out of the house. That's why I named him Jefferson, because he's such an individual. His favorite perch is on the table near the front door. He can see out the window from there. The table is supposed to be for mail and dropping bags on whenever I return home, but Jefferson has commandeered it."

Lanie had baked Gruyère cheese pinwheels and Eric, sitting on Lanie's old couch across from her, picked a feather out of one pinwheel point.

"Baked in?" laughed Lanie. "That happens. Another sip of wine will kill whatever came with it."

Eric tried to laugh off finding the unwanted ingredient. He thought about the mites and bacteria that could be crawling on those feathers. Lanie's birds were ignoring him, but they lighted on Lanie now and then, usually her shoulders. They liked to pick up strands of her hair and then let them drop.

"That's old music," Eric commented on the background sounds, wanting to forget the feather.

"Sixties and seventies is still my favorite, all those college albums."

"Albums … haven't heard that word for a while," said Eric.

"Let me take you to my studio," offered Lanie, rising from her grandmother's checkered cloth chair. Eric followed her down a narrow hall. "Of course it's just a second bedroom," she said entering the small room to the right, "but one of the reasons I rented this house was because I could manipulate the space artistically. This room gets a good deal of light, so I can move between this environment and the open kitchen area, following the sun's rays."

Lanie sat in front of her easel for him and one of the birds flew to pose on a corner, as if waiting for its portrait to be painted.

"This one is Sprite. She's sweet. There's a Spite around here, too, named Spite for obvious reasons."

Though it was after five o'clock in the evening, Eric imagined Lanie drenched in morning sunlight in front of the easel. He wanted to kiss her.

Lanie continued talking, rising from the chair, oblivious to her possible charms. "I fixed the molding around this window recently where it had rotted away," she pointed. "I also recently bought a new dishwasher for the kitchen."

"For a rental?" Eric asked. "Did the owners pay you back?"

"Well, no, in fact they don't even know—yet. I guess one day when I leave we'll have a discussion and work things out."

"That's pretty casual of you, and generous," Eric added.

Over the years Lanie had done a lot of the home's needed repairs herself or else she contracted someone to complete them without informing the owners. She wanted to be liked as a tenant.

"Out there," Lanie pointed beyond the window's glass, "I'd like to start a garden next spring. I'm too late this year as we're halfway through summer."

Lanie said the same thing to herself every year, that she would grow a garden, but she never did.

Several of the birds liked the window as well and seemed to create a fluttering halo around Lanie's head. Eric heard her listing birds' names: Penny, Amelia, Dot, and Lolita ... Benny, Pix, and Tonton ...

Eric walked to a small set of bookshelves against another wall. "These can't still be your college textbooks."

"They are. Can't seem to discard them. They contain so many notes. I put so much time into those books."

"But do you ever read them?" Eric asked as he browsed the titles. "Now I mean?"

"Not the textbooks, but I do reread the literature books—Shakespeare, Hemingway, Dickinson, Whitman. All the biggies." Lanie seemed defensive.

"Sherwood Anderson, the author, do you remember him?"

"Sure, he wrote *Winesburg, Ohio*. All those people stuck in the little town of inertia. Only George gets out at the book's end. Then in the last scene he's almost stuck in a painting himself. I wonder if he ever got out of Winesburg for real," Lanie asked wistfully.

"Do you read current authors?"

"I'm afraid I don't read much of anything that's written today," she admitted.

Lanie read no global news, just the hometown newspaper that arrived free twice a week. She knew what was on sale at the local groceries and who ran for town council; however, she rarely followed up by paying attention to the council's decisions. She frequently missed the evening news and refused to pay for cable TV, preventing a cultural or political awareness from sources the likes of CNN or even Fox. In the morning and while painting she listened only to music and her birds.

And despite her narrow life Eric liked Lanie very much. He saw in her such potential and sensitivity. He wanted to remove her from the house, remove her from the town, in order to display to her the world. He wanted to rip her from her small canvas of a life where she painted familiar landscapes in warm hues and yank her across distant spaces where she would have to negotiate rocks and holes and hard places—all with him. He wanted her to feel pain, the kind that indoctrinates, and then let him save her through discussion and merging. He wanted to watch her absorb the world. He wanted to remove her from the inertia of *Winesburg, Ohio*.

And then one of Lanie's clocks chimed in, breaking the silence to announce the six o'clock hour. Eric startled. And then another clock did the same. And soon three, and then four, and then an untold number of clocks were striking 6 P.M. The chiming sounds emanated from every room, some resounding more like a cacophony of Chinese gongs through the walls.

"I always know what time it is around here," smiled Lanie.

"What's with all the clocks?" asked Eric, his voice raised.

"I've just collected them." Lanie spoke as though oblivious to the discord.

"You can't collect time," he shouted now as the din rose. "You've got to spend time."

"Let's move back into the kitchen where it's quieter." Lanie waited for the last clock to cease. "I can shoo the birds in here," and she deftly guided them into a big cage opposite her easel. Somehow the creatures listened and obediently occupied the space.

.   .   .

Eric decided Lanie could have been a master chef. The combination of carmelized onions, stewed tomatoes, and cheeses she whipped up for him—not even begun yet when they had toured the studio—tasted better than anything he could recently remember. Lanie proved to be quite the baker as well, filling whatever corner of his stomach could possibly still be empty with a German chocolate upside down cake.

On any day of the week Lanie could be found baking and then she gave away the food as gifts to people she hardly knew—strawberry tarts to the clerk at the bank, a cheese torte to the mechanic who added fluid to her car at no charge, cranberry muffins to the librarian from whom she checked out books, bread to the owner of a pottery store—but she confused the recipients by refusing any sort of social invitation, however small, to those she had been bribing. And it was bribery. Such interactions allowed her to tell her brother on the phone, for instance, how she had "shared" her bread with a fellow artist—the pottery store owner she hardly knew and who had merely *received* the bread with warm surprise rather than *shared* it with her. And of course Bella received so much she had to quietly discard what became moldy or stale—all the while on the lookout for feathers. Lanie's baked gifts seemed to be saying, "Don't forget me."

That night Lanie was certain she was falling in love with Eric. She had not had a relationship in a very long time. During college she had lived with two different men, one who had wanted marriage and a second who had cheated on her. She said no to the marriage proposal and goodbye to the philanderer; yet over the years she had forgotten neither man. She wanted to contact them, one to forgive the cheating and the other to congratulate him on his marriage. Bella had called the idea idiotic since both men had moved on, likely had families, and besides, "That was like eons ago. They've progressed, but you're still living your college life, so you can't imagine what that's like, how you would interfere. No wife is going to understand your innocent inquiries."

Lanie admitted to Bella that she had looked both men up online. It had been easy given their prominent positions, one a biologist in the state and the other active in politics.

"I might just write them short letters. Maybe an email," suggested Lanie tentatively.

"That would be dis-*sas*-ter-ous," answered Bella. "You have no idea what feelings could follow. Your former boyfriends are likely to ignore you, making you feel isolated." *More isolated* thought Bella. "Also, there's always the possibility of the wife's wrath, creating the need for an apology on your part and *further* unwarranted contact. Plus, your own feelings will get even more stirred up than they are at this moment. And nothing can be done about those. *Noth*-ing."

But her feelings right now were all for Eric, and he taught her to lay her paintbrushes aside and explore places outside of the house she had shut herself away from. She learned to close her front door and worry less about the birds. She began to paint without their inclusion. She fairly abandoned her kitchen and ate at restaurants with Eric, places of his choosing. He taught her to give in to temptation, to take risks, and to say yes. Once, as fall approached, the two sat on the balcony of The Charm of India restaurant watching as the sun set and sketched next summer's garden on a large napkin they had asked for just for that purpose. Lanie folded the paper like a towel and sequestered it away deep into the pocket of her jacket, but before Eric left after dropping her home that evening, he asked for the sketch, folding it flat, and hung it with magnets to the refrigerator's door. "That's your future, Lanie. Growth."

And over the winter they kept one another warm and even went away together on two separate weekends. Lanie learned to understand her staleness, her stasis, as Eric made life new and real. Lanie told no one about her romance, but she had stopped loitering in the restaurant and the former card store downtown, and enjoyed shopping in the new boutiques and markets. Her paintings lost their sentimental hues and she used vibrant colors and sharp strokes instead. She gave several of the birds to a nearby school who had advertised for reasonably sized pets the children could learn to responsibly take care of, and many of her clocks remained unwound. She discarded the tattered old sofa and even her grandmother's chair. Most of her clothes from the seventies and eighties were donated to Goodwill or left on consignment at the local vintage store. The old double bed had been replaced with a firm queen soon after meeting Eric.

And then one day as winter approached Eric appeared at her front door, his face stricken, molded into an expression she knew was not from the cold but for her benefit. By now she didn't need to sense his mood, she knew it.

"What's wrong?"

"Let's sit down."

The two sat beside one another on the edge of Lanie's recently purchased couch, their knees touching. Lanie's nerves became electrified, especially where her left knee connected with Eric's right. However, the sensation felt foreign. Even the remaining birds hushed.

"You know I travel a good deal for work and I've got to do it again," began Eric.

Lanie relaxed. "I can deal with that. How long will you be gone?"

Eric hesitated. "Months ... maybe years."

Lanie froze.

"They want me ... and I want me ... I mean I want myself ... I mean I *want* to move to London." He knew he was talking too fast. He took Lanie's hands in his. "And I want you to come with me, Lanie. I'm asking you to marry me. I know it's sudden and utterly unromantic, but I don't want to leave without you."

"But you would, yes?" asked Lanie, almost in a whisper. She stared at the bold burnt orange of the new couch, suddenly pining for the faded tan plaid of the old one. She remembered how smart one of her college dresses, now hanging for sale at Once Again Vintage Love on Main Street downtown had looked with the black leggings she currently wore. Eric saw that her eyes had taken on the rheumy look of a basset hound and he feared she would begin crying.

"Don't say it that way. Take a day or two to decide. I know that's not much time either. But this London thing came up very recently, although I'll admit I resisted telling you until all the details were finalized. I can leave when I want, but they'd really like me there within the month."

"A month." Lanie seemed to be speaking from within a tunnel that had developed in her head. "Just what would I do with the birds? The house?"

"The birds don't matter. The rest can go to that school you gave the first group to. And you don't even own this house."

As soon as the words came out of his mouth he regretted them.

Lanie's entire demeanor had changed.

"I don't mean that the birds and the house don't matter," Eric backpedaled. "I know they matter to you."

"But they obviously don't matter to you."

How would he recover? "You could give the birds to Bella. Then you'd know they were safe. She could write you letters about the birds, about their progress." Bird progress? Eric hardly knew what he was saying. "I've taught you to say yes to opportunities, Lanie. Please say yes to me. Have I taught you to say yes to me?"

She promised she would consider the idea, the change. Eric told her he didn't like her use of *consider*, that by now he hoped she would feel more confidence in their relationship.

One of the variegated lovebirds alighted onto Lanie's right shoulder and tugged at her hair. Its partner flew to perch on the back of the couch between Lanie and Eric, as if mounting a defense. Eric could never keep the birds' names straight. From across the room Jefferson eyed Eric from his usual roost near the front entrance. As Eric left, Jefferson made no attempt to escape through the open door.

.   .   .

Two weeks later Lanie sat down before her easel. Usually the bird's presence in the painting had to grow organically since it could be placed in any one of a hundred spots.

Today, she sketched the bird in first.

WHAT REMAINS

After Tom's death Evelyn recycled. She dealt with her husband's loss in the only way she knew how, by planning, organizing, and dispatching. It made her feel better. She hadn't been doing away with Tom's possessions. She was moving them ... forward. She wasn't going to be one of those wives who kept a museum-like closet of mute suits for so long they would never have fit her husband even if he were to miraculously return to life. Plus, she had had enough of incommunicative men in dark suits during Tom's hospital stay.

One day Evelyn would be cremated. She had thought her urn would be added to Tom's coffin, cradled in his left arm, as they had slept in life, but he had been adamant about his body being cremated as well. "Can't have anything left," he had said one night. She might have asked what he meant, but they were young and death was but a distant thought. In the meantime Evelyn painted two walls of the kitchen a deep purple because Tom had once called it his favorite color on her. After the funeral she also moved out of their bedroom into the spare room across the second-floor hall, unable to endure the lack of Tom's physical presence. But then she moved back after two weeks, unable to live with the blank walls and lack of memories formed in a room given over to guests.

Over time she learned to live with Tom's absence as his presence. Tom's body had been put in the ground, he was gone, she knew that, but his vacuum became so palpable it grew to exist, and Evelyn began to live more comfortably with her husband's material vacancy.

.   .   .

Even before Tom's death, Evelyn was afraid of death, of course, but she was also afraid of getting breast cancer, crossing in front of a parked car, believing it would suddenly rev forward to crush her, and catching the Avian bird flu virus. Her husband's pancreatic cancer fit into these uncontrollable mysteries of life.

Tom's physical changes had begun with the simple act of getting up. And that's the way he had put it, this man with a doctorate in communications began communicating with an uncharacteristic simplicity. One early April he complained for the first time. "It's hard to get up, Evie. It hurts to walk." Sometimes he had mid back pain, sometimes abdominal pain. He decided to disregard it, though he and Evelyn tried all the home remedies that naturally come to the adult mind when dealing with annoying discomfort. Tom lay in a warm tub and then on the bed with pillows under his knees. Everyone over fifty has back pain he reasoned. Hell, everyone over thirty-five has back pain. And what's a little stomach upset? Over the next two months, he took an antacid now and then. And he enjoyed instead the fact that he had lost ten pounds effortlessly.

His first visit to Dr. Ernst resulted in no clear answer. Tom was barely over fifty, didn't smoke, drank only socially, exercised, and was in relatively good health for his age. He was doing what so many active baby boomers do: ignoring the pain, hoping it would go away. Later that day Dr. Ernst would describe Tom's pain as "nonspecific" on his patient's medical chart, a seemingly careless encapsulation of the exam to a nonphysician, but one which indicated Ernst's nervousness regarding Tom's symptoms. Tom had no acute pain, yet his complaints attested to more than simple discomfort. Did eating make the pain better or worse asked Ernst. Does the pain wake you up at night? He ordered blood tests to check for the anemia of a bleeding ulcer. It would come back normal. Ernst saw no pattern to Tom's complaints, and the unexplained weight loss increased the physician's concerns. He saw a man losing vigor.

"The pain is just dull," said Tom somewhat lifelessly.

Ernst prescribed continued antacids as needed as well as Prilosec to get rid of the acid in Tom's stomach. He asked Tom to do nothing to confuse the picture. "Don't aggravate the situation by trying your best friend's surefire home remedy," he warned. Most of all, Tom was to monitor his symptoms closely. The physician also requested his patient schedule another appointment in two weeks.

The next time Dr. Ernst saw Tom, he was already in the hospital. The night before he had gone to bed sometime before 11 P.M. with the usual discomfort, but lying down had made the pain grow greater than usual. At 11:15 P.M. he asked Evelyn to stop bouncing the bed when she had only been reading. At midnight, his wife asleep, Tom was suffering. At 12:56 A.M. he woke Evelyn and asked her to take him to the hospital.

"Now?" she asked sleepily.

"*Now.*"

They arrived at the emergency room just before 2 A.M. "We've got to do some imaging," soon concluded the attending physician, and because even at that hour of the morning the machine was still "warm," as the staff put it, Tom was sent for a CT, or computed tomography scan. Clearly demonstrating more than minimal illness, within a short time Tom was admitted to the hospital. He needed not just relief but a diagnosis.

Dr. Ernst met a shaken Tom and Evelyn the next morning. By then Tom had been moved to a private room where he lay with his head and back elevated slightly at his request. Evelyn stood at her husband's right side, the window overlooking the parking lot with the mountains behind her. Dr. Ernst stood on Tom's left side, facing Evelyn. Tom appeared as colorless as the sheets on his bed and wore a faded green hospital gown decorated with equally dim random black circles which swirled and disappeared into themselves. He, too, seemed to be vanishing into the gown's excess material.

The three greeted one another, but given the circumstances and the look on the couple's faces, the physician got to the point.

"Tom, are you having night pain? Is that what brought you here last night?"

"Oh, God, yes. That's become the worst. Unrelenting."

"So you're feeling much worse than the last time I saw you?" asked Ernst, purposely repeating Tom's term.

"Sometimes words can't even describe the pain, especially at night."

"Can you try? Words, I mean. Can you try to put it in words for me?

Asked to think now rather than grimace from pain, Tom had to clear his head. "It's gnawing," he finally said. "But it's visceral. Don't ask me where it really is. And I feel like an anorexic. Sometimes I vomit."

"So you feel nausea too," Ernst confirmed. "The attending physician last night noted the pain as mid-back. Would you still agree?

"Yes," said Tom weakly.

The physician looked at his stoic patient and wondered how balanced he would remain. Earlier that morning Ernst had stopped in to see the radiologist who, due to the start of the day, had not yet read Tom's CT results.

"Will you take a look?" Ernst had asked.

The radiologist's initial conclusions were at once negative. "Looks like pancreatic CA, Ron." Then he pointed, "And there's a bony erosion."

"Damn."

.   .   .

"I've received a verbal CT scan report from the radiologist, Tom." Ernst wavered a scant second. "It's not good. It's showing you've got bone erosion at the spine."

Evelyn paled and gripped Tom's hand. Tom froze and stared ahead as if awaiting a cue to relax.

"This is quite serious. And I'm afraid I can't rule out something cancerous at this point."

Evelyn emitted an involuntary sound that was cut short when it became stuck at the back of her throat.

"How—?" whispered Tom, his words curtailed as well.

Ernst continued his explanation in order to fill in the canyon of silence that was developing across the bed between himself and the couple.

"There's a lump in your upper abdomen. It's sitting next to your spine and has made bony changes in your spine."

Ernst used his balled hands pushed up against one another to demonstrate, but in their state of disbelief Tom and Evelyn saw no connection between the physician's visible hands and Tom's hidden bones.

Tom tried clearing his throat several times. His words gurgled, draining away as he asked in a choked voice, "Where—"

Tom swallowed.

"Where is the lump growing ... if it is?"

"The pancreas, Tom."

.   .   .

If Tom did have pancreatic cancer, he didn't fit the profile. Ernst encountered the cancer infrequently in his practice, perhaps once a year. Yet the last case had been recent, a man in his seventies who had quickly died. But Tom was barely over fifty. Plus, pancreatic cancer was two to three times more common in smokers, and Tom didn't smoke. At one time coffee had been thought to be a factor, but subsequent research had shown no correlation. In fact, pancreatic cancer had no firm cause. Ernst, therefore, had no reassuring words for Tom and Evelyn. What he did know was that if Tom had a pancreatic tumor, it was quite likely malignant. Ninety-five percent of afflicted patients died. As cancers went, it was one of the worst. It was rarely cured.

.   .   .

In the hospital room Evelyn felt she could hardly stand. She wondered where her legs and feet were. She wasn't hearing the doctor properly. Her ears seemed to have folded and dissolved into her brain. She tried forming a logical question in order to locate herself in the room again. She asked feebly, "What does the pancreas even do, Dr. Ernst?"

The physician had been standing straight and tall, but he, too, had had to shift his body in order to displace some of the emotional discomfort in the room, but the question alleviated his own unease, allowing him to talk on a factual level rather than an emotional level.

"Well, its function is to make digestive juices but it also makes hormones, one to increase blood sugar, and another to decrease blood sugar." He saw that Tom and Evelyn were listening to him but he didn't know how much of what he said they let in. "One to increase and one to decrease," he repeated. "Go figure, in one organ." The Saunders did not react to this physiological puzzle. Ernest tried again. "The pancreas is behind the stomach, which makes the back pain. That's what you're feeling so acutely."

The couple was trying to process the information, but Ernst knew they couldn't.

"And I'm sure you're also both feeling a great deal of confusion overall right now," he acknowledged.

"Confusion," repeated Evelyn tonelessly. She put her hands to her face, her palms pressing against her cheeks. She looked somewhat ridiculous, but she didn't know it and she certainly wouldn't have cared.

Ernst waited to see if he should go on.

Tom cleared his throat. "Are you sure about this?" he asked in a surprisingly strong voice.

Dr. Ernst removed his arm from the table and lay a reassuring hand on Tom's shoulder. "I'm not sure of anything yet, Tom. We'll do some further tests and poking around first." He made ready to leave the couple, eager to be free of the room's restrictions and seeming lack of oxygen.

Tom suddenly turned and in a loud but cracked voice asked, "So what are you saying, Doc? Give it to me straight." He summoned up the anemic smile of artificial courage.

But the physician was circumspect. "I'm not saying anything yet, Tom."

*　　*　　*

Ernst read the radiologist's report. Tom's malignancy measured four centimeters and included lymph node involvement as well as the bony erosion. Ernst later told Tom his prognosis was "quite poor," but it was in fact very bad. Pancreatic cancer was twice as common in the head of the pancreas as in the body or tail, but Tom's cancer was located in the tail. Had it been in the head, Tom's bile duct likely would have closed some time ago, the resulting jaundice an alert sending Tom for imaging sooner. Instead, his cancer had been given a chance to grow silently, without any message heralding its existence.

Tom would not go home. Not only did he need a good deal of morphine to reach any degree of temporary comfort, but the hospital environment allowed the easy hook up of IVs for nourishment, countering Tom's developing resistance to food.

When they were more prepared, Ernst discussed medical options with the couple.

"We can send you to Duke where they could have people with particular knowledge, people with more sophistication in this area. They may be doing some cutting-edge procedure I'm unaware of.

Tom looked grim.

"Radiation—chemotherapy—they can be tried too, but these procedures mean going to a Class A institution also."

"A research hospital then," said Evelyn.

"Yes," confirmed Ernst, but given Evelyn's strain, he didn't know if she was endorsing the idea or dismissing it. With the prior case of his elderly patient, Ernst had gone to the latest medical journals, and statistics and conclusions remained in his head. "In the right place and working with the right people, patients with pancreatic cancer have lived up to thirty-two months."

"Less than three years," lamented Tom, while Evelyn's simultaneous response signaled a modicum of hope: "Almost three years," she said plainly, as though choosing between items as ordinary as butter and margarine. *I'll take the butter, please.* Ernst could hear that Tom and his wife were not yet thinking alike concerning the future. But how could they?

"The median patient, however," clarified Ernst, "lives eleven months."

The three contemplated this statistic to differing degrees.

"Doc, enough," broke Tom. "I'm tired of lying here—contemplating. What do I need to do? Can't you operate? Operate *here?*"

Ernst knew the location of the tumor impacted heavily on post-operative survival. Moreover, four of five with pancreatic cancer at the time of diagnosis were unresectable, in other words, inoperable. Of those who did have surgery with curative intent, the five-year survival rate was just twenty percent.

Tom suspected, even as he asked, that his request was a hollow one.

.   .   .

Tom was dead. But Evelyn was breathing air again, not air that seemed to come from pumps and mechanical monsters within a stifling hospital room, but real air outside the hospital's walls, air polluted with carbons and soot and natural bacterias—but not with sickness and death.

The two men approached her as she left through the building's front entrance. They wore suits and dark sunglasses. She had seen them before. She quickened her step.

"Dr. Saunders, may we speak with you?" the taller of the two called out as he advanced toward her. "Just a quick word, please."

Evelyn stopped cold on the sidewalk, just as she was about to step down onto the black asphalt of the visitors' parking lot. *Whatever this is, let's get it over with.*

"We're sorry about the loss of your husband, ma'am," said the same tall man.

Evelyn did not react.

"Could we ask you to sit down?" He indicated a nearby bench a few feet away.

"No," she answered tartly.

"Ma'am, I'll make this quick," said the shorter of the two men, moving in as if his partner were taking too much trouble with his affected manners. "We need to ask you if Tom said anything at the end, just prior to his death."

"What?"

"This is important, ma'am."

"Gentleman, I don't know who you are, but my husband just died and I am going home." With one foot Evelyn attempted to take a step off the sidewalk.

"Ma'am," tried the taller one again, "we worked with your husband."

Evelyn planted her foot back on the cement. "My husband worked at Wendell, and by the looks of you two, you don't. Now please leave me alone or I'll call hospital security."

"Ma'am, we work for NCIC," explained the shorter man, his tone becoming more conciliatory, "the North Carolina Institute of Communication. It's a branch."

"It's a branch of what?"

"It's a branch of the government."

"My husband worked for the state, not the government."

As if on cue, each man reached into his jacket and from a hidden breast pocket pulled out a black wallet, the interior of which revealed a photo identity card proving government affiliation.

"We do security work," said the shorter of the two in a practiced way as if the line were their standard dodge.

Evelyn did not believe him. "This is ridiculous. My husband never mentioned you or the NCIT."

"NCIC, ma'am," corrected the taller man, "North Carolina Institute of Communication."

"So what are you, CIA, FBI?" Evelyn asked sarcastically.

The men looked straight at her without answering.

Evelyn became worried. Had Tom been mixed up in something? Why wouldn't he have told her? She became flustered. She clutched her purse across her chest as though she feared a theft. "So what do you want from me?"

The taller of the men continued, "We need to know what Tom said at the end, just prior to his death. His words may not have seemed important at the time. They will mean more to us." He again urged her to move to the bench.

"How dare you imply that you know more ... I am *not* sitting. I am leaving." She endeavored to move right, then left, uselessly rocking, in an attempt to get around one or the other of the two men, but they appeared too dark and looming. She stopped her efforts, swallowed, and undertook to speak forcefully. "Listen, I don't know what you're talking about and I certainly am not going to divulge private deathbed conversations to two thugs I've never met."

The taller of the two men tried again, undeterred. "Could he—"

"His name was *Tom*," snarled Evelyn.

"Excuse me. Could Tom have mentioned anything about particular numbers, for instance, repeating numbers? Or perhaps a place called Highcoate?"

"Of course not. I can hardly make anything out of your jargon and innuendo myself—numbers, Highcomb, NC whatever. This conversation is absurd. You're speaking another language." Evelyn was becoming quite anxious and her tone became high and griping. Some on the sidewalk were beginning to look at the three.

"Anything you can remember could have great potential." The shorter of the men was not backing down either.

"For *whom*?" Evelyn demanded.

The taller man tried to comfort her. "We don't mean to alarm you, Dr. Saunders," he said in a low voice.

"Well, you're doing a wonderful job of it."

"We're sorry. And thank you for your time."

And then the men had walked away, the bewildering interrogation over.

.   .   .

The two men had made reference to Tom's potential. Though she felt she remembered every word each had said to her outside the hospital's walls, Evelyn had never been able to piece the event together. Helpful for whom? Did Tom have the potential to help the men? The government? The so-called NCIC? Evelyn herself? Why hadn't Tom told her of his involvement? And in what? Was he really involved? She had seen the men's badges that day, but in her state of mind she had read the names without retaining them. Had the two men mistaken her for someone else? Mistaken Tom for someone else?

She had first seen the men in the Intensive Care Unit during the last days of Tom's life. Maybe it was the last hours ... Maybe she couldn't remember everything anymore. She had been in the hallway outside the unit, Tom having fallen asleep again. She heard snippets of the men's conversations with the nurse in charge—*We would like to speak to ... Here are our credentials from ... It's important that this not be broadcast*—but she had paid little attention to the murmurs at the time. Exhausted, when she did lean forward to take a languid glance at the understated commotion, she had looked right through the men, sensing only the incongruity of their dark suits and sunglasses. Had she even heard Tom's name mentioned?

The head nurse had been adamant, however. No entrance without a release from the patient himself. Not even physicians themselves make changes here. The men were turned away. They accepted the woman's refusal with aplomb and walked toward the floor's elevator doors, already opening as if ready to remove the men at the head nurse's first demand. Once within the interior of the elevator, the taller of the two men turned toward Evelyn, not taking his eyes off the grieving woman until the doors shut.

Evelyn had not noticed. She had found a chair and was trying to doze amidst the smell of death.

.   .   .

If Tom really had been involved with the NCIC, why had he not told her? What else had he not told her? Why had she had to learn such information, if it were even true, from two men in dark suits whose eyes she couldn't even see? Evelyn contemplated her long marriage. She had always been happy. How could she then be unhappy about being married—considering technically she was no longer married?

How was she to view her union with Tom? Twenty-five years ... ten thousand assurances ... assurances that had suddenly lost weight. Were they two people who had met, merged, and merely formed a kind of utilitarian affiliation? What had become of all Evelyn had confided? Every utterance Tom had ever made now seemed more like an unheeded warning rather than an act of faith.

She sat with the urn containing Tom's ashes in her lap, its lid on the table beside her. The weight of the container's marble-like pedestal cut into her thighs. She tipped the urn from side to side, but the look of the contents never changed. Balancing the vessel against her left hand, she slowly brought the tip of her right finger to her mouth, parted her lips, and then slightly brushed her tongue. Lowering the moist finger into the container's neck, she softly touched Tom's remains. His dust clung to her fingertip. She brought the finger back to her already parted lips, touched her tongue again, and, like Artemisia, became her husband's living tomb.

Then Evelyn divided herself from her marriage.

THE BOX FROM OZ

The new husband had deposited them in the North Carolina mountain house and then left. Benjamin had not yet started school and had no companions. Moreover, his mother was occupied with her new home. The new husband worked in the banking industry, centered in Charlotte just two hours away, but he traveled around the region and could not be counted on to return regularly. "This will not be a 9-5 marriage," he warned his new wife, but he had said it with a smile and she had been up for the adventure.

Benjamin and his mother moved into the new husband's home, but his mother had claimed her new bedroom was entirely too cramped so the new husband obliged by agreeing to add a large L, lengthening the master bedroom at the back of the house and adding an office for his new wife's pleasure. The structure totaled twelve hundred square feet, "adding a house to a house" the new husband announced cheerfully, and its massive decks now stuck out pretentiously in front of the existing structure. Downstairs the basement was extended as well.

What would be done with this space he did not know, for he was without imagination beyond concrete numbers, but there it was, a consequence of love. The new husband felt the construction work would amuse his wife, a way to make at least part of the house feel more familiar to her.

Benjamin had no feeling one way or the other for the new house or the new husband. At nine he was already hardened against compassion from other men; it wasn't that he did not like them, there had just been so many of them. Of his own father he knew very little, and he still retained a vestige of hope that his real father would retrieve him one day, though he did not know how this event would occur.

Previously Benjamin had lived on an isolated bluff overlooking the Mississippi River in Dubuque, Iowa, where his morose mother had recovered from her second divorce and the river had been her son's only friend. From above he could watch for debris and march down the pitched slope to find prizes, as he called them, his water-logged river gifts. During September and October he had somersaulted down the incline in the thickly fallen leaves, arriving slightly bruised but happy at the thrill of giving himself over to the buffeting. Once at the bottom he roamed for treasure. The river's rolling swift waters were generous, once presenting him with a spool of wire caging, which he could not drag very far but used to create a kind of protective housing for his other catches. Inside he placed what he could not carry back up the bluff's incline to the house—a bicycle without tires, several buckets, cracked, but only enough to require a bit of care with his knuckles when storing smaller objects inside, a floppy hat that fit pretty well once dry, but which his mother would never have allowed him to wear in her presence, and what he was certain were the cleaned though weathered bones of a prehistoric animal. He had heard of museums in New York, Boston, and Chicago that could be interested in his find, but he had never found the right moment to approach his mother about the prospect given her sullen demeanor.

Then one day they had packed up and left the Mississippi River and all his watery riches behind.

Now Benjamin stood at the top of the North Carolina ridge that was his new backyard gazing over a ravine that fell far more sharply than he was used to in Iowa. The ridge felt too high and too steep to climb down, and while he could observe from his purchase what simply appeared to be brush below, a failed attempt at a trip down the incline through that thicket last week had emphasized its defense of mature rhododendron which towered over him and obscured his vision.

The Mississippi River had always been in a constant state of change, but the ravine appeared static. The land below simply was.

Until the day the winds came. The new husband had returned for a few days, delighting Benjamin's mother, but, keeping their heads down and their faces toward one another, they spent a great deal of time scouring blueprints at the dining room table, his mother dictating, the new husband listening.

Benjamin still had not encountered any other small boys on the street, so on fine days he hung around by the mailbox at the head of the driveway, though not enough to appear silly and undesirable as a friend. In his solitude he pictured the ravine and tried to imagine its floor had changed, that somehow it would prove to act as the Mississippi had acted. Therefore, at his mother's command during the new husband's short visit, but not without some interest, he had sat in the man's presence as he explained the vagaries and whims of the mountain's coming winds and how they would blow on and off for months, sometimes destructively, but mostly just hard. "Watch," he urged kindly, "the landscape can alter itself every day and you could lose hold of all you know." His right hand reached toward Benjamin, an attempt at forming a bond, but the boy remained remote. The new husband leaned back in his chair as before, undeterred. "We'll have to glue you to the floor," he chuckled, which sounded like the worst thing that could happen to

Benjamin. How could he stand life becoming even more fixed than it was? Instead, he would dream of radical winds that tampered with the world.

He missed the Iowa bluffs but his mother said he should be glad to live in such a nice house during such bad economic times. "How many other boys live as you do?" she asked, intending to cause some reflection in her only son's mind, but Benjamin didn't know. He knew no other boys.

Though September had arrived and he was to be home-schooled, his mother had made no effort to begin a program, all other interests dulled by the addition's progress. And so he went to stare at the bottom of the ravine behind the house. And this time to his surprise there stood a boy, a real boy, practically illuminated by a single beam of sunshine. He strutted back and forth with purpose, unaware of Benjamin's eyes eagerly trained upon him. And a short distance away from the boy Benjamin saw part of a great box, apparently uncovered of its leaves by the tremendous winds the new husband had warned of. The box was a brilliant orange in the dappled sun and its sides seemed to glitter as if covered by tiny jewels. It threw off reds and yellows and golds. Of course the jewels must be quite large, Benjamin reasoned, given that he stood so far away at the top of the ravine.

"Hey!" yelled Benjamin down to the boy.

The boy below only slightly turned his head, not sure he had really heard a call in the deceiving wind.

"Hey! Up here!" shouted Benjamin again.

This time the boy turned, saw him, and waved, which was all Benjamin needed to begin his slide down the ravine. Without trepidation he discovered a path. All one had to do was venture out. It was not easy, but he lowered himself here to pass under a branch and there to push through the thick rhododendron growth. He closed his eyes periodically and endured scratches without complaint, and before he knew it he emerged from the dense rhododendron, only to tumble to his knees and then fall over on his side some ten feet from the boy. The boy had heard him coming and waited patiently, even with some evident anticipation. He did not even laugh at Benjamin's awkward entrance to their friendship.

"Do you live here?" asked Benjamin, rather breathless and working to stand while brushing debris from his pants.

"Way up there," pointed the boy, though Benjamin could not discern any specific location up on the ridge.

More importantly, "What's in the box over there?" Benjamin inquired.

"Not much of a box yet," admitted the boy though he said it without lament. "We're gonna have to dig it out. See how it's got itself deep in the dirt? I only saw it today."

"Me too," said Benjamin, pleased at the boy's use of *we*.

The boys were barely taller than their find. Arms spread wide, they could not have reached each end.

"Half of it's buried, like treasure. So I'm deputizing you right here on this spot."

Benjamin wasn't sure what deputizing meant but it sounded important.

"I think it's covered in jewels," he offered, wondering if the new boy would find him witless and shoo him away.

The two boys stared at the colossal container, the sunlight dancing across its visible sides, the dirt covering its promises.

"I'm Jake," the boy said proudly.

"I'm Benjamin," he returned.

The two boys shook hands.

"And this," Jake spoke as though he were a circus ringleader, "is the box from Oz."

.   .   .

Benjamin's work with Jake was progressing nicely. No side of the jeweled tank was yet fully visible, but the boys were not discouraged. They worked afternoons, pointing and gesturing with what they felt was mature resolve, slowly shoveling the packed and unyielding dirt away from the sides of the giant box until their small arms protested too much, and then leaned against tree trunks with their arms across their chests, all the while evaluating like men at a construction site the best way to pull what had come to feel like a kind of structure out of the ground and fully to light.

"Maybe there's a wizard inside who can ..." Jake winked. He didn't finish his thought, but each boy knew since they were so alike.

Benjamin was not sure what Jake's aim was concerning the shiny case once unearthed, or his own for that matter, but when their best efforts caused the jewels to loosen and fall to the ground, Benjamin retrieved them, wishing he still had use of his abandoned Mississippi buckets for storage. As he worked to separate the pieces and combine those of like color, the flakes sometimes broke again between his fingers, becoming just flecks. His mother liked gems. Prior to her marriage, after just a three-month courtship, the new husband had presented Benjamin's mother with a diamond necklace and soon after a bracelet with glittering green stones. Benjamin knew that with a little thought he could devise a way to fashion jewelry for his mother from his collection, causing her to again find his company more desirable than that of the new husband.

But now such gifts had stopped as the house project had grown. Benjamin knew this because his mother had complained to her own mother one rainy afternoon while Benjamin had listened surreptitiously to their phone conversation from the floor of the dark kitchen pantry. He had been there hiding out from Blackbeard himself who apparently, despite his death in 1718, had made the cross-state trek from his sunken ship off the coast of Beaufort Inlet, North Carolina, to spend necessary playtime with Benjamin.

"Did my father like adventure?" asked Benjamin one day of his mother out of the blue.

"Your ... *father*? Well, yes, I suppose so, perhaps a bit too much." She had always tried to be honestly evasive with Benjamin regarding her first marriage. The second she avoided discussing altogether.

"I mean like pirates."

"Pirates? Aren't you too old to be thinking of pirates? Does this all have to do with the Oz box you talk about and that little friend of yours I've never met?"

"How much did my father know me?"

"Oh," responded his mother with wry hesitation, "I'm sure he'd find you interesting." She felt the conversation finish.

Yet, the unintentional connotation in his mother's words was all it took to set Benjamin's mind ablaze concerning his lost father. Perhaps he was lonely somewhere and needed him. He wished he could tell his father about the jeweled vessel, about his friend Jake, about treasures found and lost, and then found again in new forms. He wanted his father to know he could return, that life worked like that, if you dreamed forward enough.

.   .   .

Benjamin could see his mother tiring of the new husband already. His constant travel annoyed her and the construction crew seemed to arrive randomly, on its own kind of intermittent schedule. In a vain attempt at garnering some sympathetic attention, she claimed she was afraid to be in the house alone with the workers. "I'm from Iowa," she protested, forgetting she had lived in many areas of the country. "I don't know about Mexicans."

"You have to say Hispanics now, love," said the new husband, "and plenty of Hispanics live in Iowa, too."

But over time she became quite interested in the workers, welcoming them on their periodic arrivals, even making a nuisance of herself amongst them. Sometimes a whole crew came to work; sometimes just one man. She began to bring them drinks and sweet treats from the kitchen.

"Oh, *again*, Mrs. Teak," said the embarrassed foreman. "Why ... thank you."

"Call me Carole," she had said.

She had added the *e* to her name in college to feel elegant and mature. Any legal signature omitted the letter, though she had tried to sign her latest marriage certificate using the *e*. Luckily her husband had caught the error or the license might have been void he warned.

Soon one worker in particular began showing up on days when the rest of the crew did not. Benjamin's mother would walk down the long dark hallway, having secured her son's interest elsewhere, open the door to the swelling master bedroom, which momentarily lit up the end of the hallway, and then close the door behind her.

Later she became more careless. One day Benjamin was halfway down the hallway behind her in his silent socked feet, his mother so close but seeming already insubstantial until she disappeared behind the whoosh of the door, blown away like dust.

.   .   .

The late October winds assaulted Benjamin's face and ears, distorting sound. Leaves whirled around him, settled, and then whirled even more violently. The ravine was in constant motion now and the Mississippi had faded in Benjamin's mind.

While busy with the work of digging, Benjamin had begun to contemplate how the box had landed at the bottom of the ravine. Maybe some boy ... or a group of boys, boys older and with more muscle in their arms, laughing and enjoying themselves, not solitary as he was ... perhaps with their arms lazily draped around one another's broad shoulders ... had collectively decided to kick ... no push the tank to the edge of the ridge into the ravine below. In his mind he watched it tumble down the incline now and heard the satisfaction in the boys' shouts to one another.

Only once during the digging had someone walked by, a hiker who gave Benjamin a wave and moved on. Benjamin hadn't heard the man approaching as the wind had turned all sound into one, masking the traveler's footsteps over the ravine's floor. Benjamin brought forth a short "Hello," but Jake said nothing, seemingly disconnected by their discovery's secrets. Benjamin had felt nearly the same paralysis. He knew it could be seen as foolish to deal in wizards and treasures. And yet the box stayed afloat in his head. He no longer even minded being sent to bed alone. The golden box lit up his dreams.

·　　·　　·

The previous day Benjamin had overheard an argument between his mother and the new husband over his frequent absences. "But I've got a chance to …" Benjamin didn't hear the rest, because the two had moved into another room and behind a door, but somehow he already understood the adult world of ambition and human separation.

The Hispanic crew member who had caught his mother's attention was soon released. Benjamin had heard the foreman's scolding tone and seen the other man's hands up in the air in an empty gesture of defeat. The two men had stood in the driveway late one afternoon as Benjamin had returned from the ravine. Little had been completed and the foreman was tired of the crew member's excuses.

In the days after the man's dismissal, his mother just sat.

"Would he ever come find us?"

His mother turned from her vacant stare through the dining room window toward the ravine to focus on her son. "Would *who* ever come find us?"

"My father."

Carol Teak pulled her son closer and ran her fingers through his hair.

"Maybe that could be nice," she said in a faraway voice.

.   .   .

In the ensuing weeks the adult world around him argued, mired in a state of rearranging. And Mrs. Teak soon found another worker to help make the minutes pass.

In addition, Jake had not appeared for days. Still, Benjamin worked to uncover the box. Perhaps Jake had a father who had suddenly needed him.

And then a group of five older boys appeared from nowhere down in Benjamin's ravine, strolling toward him with the confidence of those playing hooky and not yet caught. The boys, lanky and loose-limbed, had not yet grown into their bodies. The seeming leader of the group, the tallest, meant no harm and was almost solicitous to Benjamin when he spoke.

With a bit of a smirk he asked the boy before him what he was doing. Benjamin remained evasive except to say that Jake had helped him dig. He felt uncertain about the older and bigger boys and wanted to imply human support, though Benjamin was beginning to doubt Jake's existence.

Collectively the older boys claimed there was "no Jake around here." Leaves bombarded them and swirled below around their feet, the ravine's vain protective attempt to admonish the group.

The sun had left, now tucked in the clouds, and before the boys the box had lost its luster, the jewels turning to rust.

"I'm afraid what you got there is a septic tank, kid," spoke up the leader again. Now the other boys ridiculed Benjamin.

"It's a *septic tank*," said one.

Benjamin stood mute, unaware of the meaning of what the boy had said.

"It's for *shit*," cried out another above the wind.

The leader ignored his minions, taking Benjamin's silence as a request for more information. He also thought the boy somewhat of an idiot. "I know because my dad works in tanks. That one's old. It's not even regulation. They don't allow metal tanks anymore, least not around here."

The other boys flanked the speaker, moving closer to him.

"Used to be they could be used if covered by a bituminous material."

The other boys looked at him. *Bituminous?*

"It waterproofs." The tall boy felt superior and paused dramatically. The wind complied, slackening.

"That's the problem. This one got too wet," he confirmed. "Material's all flaked off leaving this rusted relic."

The boys laughed at the unexpected reference to a rusted relic, but their reaction was really to conceal their embarrassment at their definition deficit. They couldn't have repeated *bituminous* to save their lives, but they had heard the word and now understood it and felt power.

"This is the county. What ain't reported ain't inspected, and what ain't inspected ain't reported." The leader of the boys crossed his arms over his chest, proud of his pronouncement.

"You're playing with shit, kid," said one of the boys from behind him, not brave enough to show his face.

"Shit for toys. What a life," scoffed another.

The wind picked up again.

And then the boys simply turned and ambled away, continuing across the ravine, periodically disappearing behind tree trunks as they became smaller and smaller and thinner and thinner until they vanished altogether, erased by a final dizzying burst of leaves as though the encounter had never happened.

.   .   .

Later at home Benjamin smiled to himself. He wasn't dejected and had recovered quickly from the boys' taunts. He had a new plan, a new story to live. He would ask his mother for the proper address later. Right now he would go to his room and write his father a letter. He walked down the long hallway and entered his bedroom. Through the window on the far wall the landscape outside appeared tumultuous, undergoing deliberate transformation. Tomorrow it would be altered again. He shut the door. He would be ready.

COMMUNITY LATITUDE

Instructor Phillip Meyers no longer felt any sexual stirrings when he stared at his student Penny Messina. She had gained weight and this semester she appeared like a blimp to him. Just ten pounds or so turned him off. As he pointed to and discerned between the various bones of the hard plastic skeleton hanging limply in front of the room, fixed plastic arrows guiding the pedagogical movement of his hands from place to place, he looked up to see Linda Landrino pass by his classroom door from the hallway. He practically frothed, lust intact.

. . .

Bunny McGuire shivered in the sunny room. Her fellow nursing students buzzed around her, swarming from task station to task station. The instructor had given them just thirty minutes to complete four of the six lessons, emphasizing that their findings must be written up *p-r-e-c-i-s-e-l-y*. They were experienced students now, about to graduate, and needed to think quickly on their feet. No mistakes could be made with actual patients in the real world. That morning Bunny had had to leave her one-year-old son Brent with his father as her mother had been unexpectedly called into work. Brent had hardly recovered from the contusions left from the last time he had stayed with Toby. Bunny felt the blows, her long sleeves and high turtleneck covering her own bruises.

.   .   .

Quentin was ready for the quiz in his history class. Roberts, Alito, Thomas, Scalia, Kennedy, Stevens, Bader Ginsburg, Sotomayor, and Breyer—he knew them all. Recently relocated to the South by his father who had taken an administrative position at the box store headquarters in town, Quentin had found southern values both curious and suspect. It was not so much that he found the views narrow; rather, they could seem off kilter. So many he met were wrapped in an incomprehensible conservative fear. He knew he would ace the quiz but continued to list the Justices out loud as he walked from the parking lot to the classroom. The first four were mnemonically easy, Roberts, Alito, Thomas, and Scalia—RATS.

.   .   .

Lud had taken ENG 111 three times with the same instructor. He had also failed each time. He pledged to his coach he would pass on the fourth try. "Pledge to *yourself*," had been the laconic response. Lud didn't even need to visit the bookstore; the texts had remained the same the past three semesters. The class would be a breeze, not because he had made the promise to his coach, but because he had done most of the reading before, even with the instructor's requirement of new essays each semester. But she sought him out a day before classes began. She used email, just as a friend of his might have, yet the tone was not the same. She used proper capitalization rather than friendly lower case. "You need to experience another instructor," she had admonished. Lud could hardly believe an instructor would make such an ignorant comment to a student. He had become quite comfortable in the class.

.   .   .

The Athletic Director had fallen for her the first time he saw her but waited a respectful Southern four months before asking her out—to a game, all he knew. His teams quickly became hers. *Administrative Assistant* read the sign at her desk, but Kayleen Drinn knew how to keep the Arts and Sciences faculty in line. Some balked at her directives, some thrived in her sanctum of efficiency. Some quailed at the sound of her voice, some reaped the rewards of her selective benevolence. For two years they all waited for her to marry the Athletic Director. But when she left to pursue her own higher degree, they felt a silent betrayal, though they could not force themselves to form the words. She deserved no blame. How could they begrudge her the very thing that drove their own lives? So they turned their emotions toward the devastated Athletic Director and grieved for him. Energy within the department became inert, the air dead, those pieces some say must be "picked up" after a loss laying as scattered debris at their feet.

.   .   .

The four sat together in a row to Tilda's right. They were quiet and pleasant enough and appeared every day in her history class, but they completed no work. They were baseball players for the school. She tried to avoid stereotyping, but she had seen it so often. They were in school only to play ball, not to study. They could not understand that in order to play ball they had to do well in school. Flunking a single class knocked them off the baseball team, an approach to sports that confused them. During the fall they had teetered in their first-semester remedial classes and now they sat precariously in spring transfer classes.

They did not know how to use the library, did not prepare the nightly readings, and spent non-field hours away from practice on Facebook. They even lived together. And so they flunked the class together and were dropped from the team together.

*   *   *

The two chefs huddled in the back row of the seated faculty who were prepared to oversee reverently the four hundred or so graduates march across the stage, one by one, to receive a coveted diploma. Those in the transfer program needed more study and, if lucky, would be off to some university for the next two years. But the culinary students were through, ready to flourish in kitchens near and far. While the rest of the faculty wore their regalia designating various universities, the two chefs were dressed in their black-on-black checked pants and white jackets, the buttons of which marched militarily in two straight rows down each side in front. Yet they felt a lack of seriousness unbecoming their profession. They had seen this day so many times before, such an important one for the graduates who donned their bakers' caps with pride, but one of personal lethargy for them as instructors who only knew the bustle of the kitchen. So they periodically passed notes between themselves and giggled like third graders. The tall white paper hat belonging to one of the chefs dropped from his lap to the floor. The other chef secretly retrieved it. He pulled a pencil from his pocket, turned slightly away from his colleague, and sketched a stickman to represent his friend. He passed the hat and his pencil to the person to his left, who added a baking pan about to drop. The next drew in what appeared to be buns flying through the air and then the cartoon was lost down the row. When the bare-headed chef was called to the lectern to announce the names of his graduates, he fumbled for his hat before noticing it waving in a fellow faculty member's hand at the row's end. He snatched it as he walked by and popped it on his head, not at all cognizant of its decorations or the fact that the pencil sketches had been deepened with a thick magic marker. The faculty behind him on the stage nearly roared as he solemnly read his students' names and shook each hand. The president of the college eyed his faculty, but his gagged reproofs did nothing to alter their mirth. At the lectern the chef bristled for he was a bear in the kitchen.

*   *   *

Praised academically by so many, she already had plans to earn a Ph.D. though she was a mere eighteen. The faculty buzzed. *There must be more than twenty years between them. Could she even cook properly? Wasn't she really just his next project? He'll discard her.* "She's an old soul," the instructor had said to the president when called into his office. "But this is a community," the president had countered, "and the community won't stand for it." The instructor disagreed. She wasn't his student; in fact, she had never even walked into his classroom—a pact they'd made—and the president was talking about his *private* life, not his faculty obligations. And so the instructor and the student were married. But contrary to prediction, she left him after less than a year, slowly recognizing the absence of what those who are young consider required experience. She wanted to tend bar. She wanted to ignore clocks. She wanted latitude. But the instructor had not fallen in love with the child. When it was over he brought some of the contents from their former kitchen cupboards to his department, including a one-pound bag of flour. His female colleagues took note its size. *Who supplies a kitchen with a one-pound bag of flour? It would be used up in no time at all.* It had been as if the girl knew.

*   *   *

The provost, tall and elegant, always straightforward with faculty, walked the hallways of the school between classes. The school had just achieved the distinction of "exceptional instructional performance," one of only a handful of community colleges in the state to do so and the only one to have won the recognition four years in a row. Yet he agonized over each cut in the state budget and fought to retain every staff and faculty position in the fall. He dreamed of building a new parking structure on the vast wasted space that was the current flat lot, but was forced to consider cutting library hours instead. He regularly balanced his aims and differences against those of the school's president and board of trustees, and he struggled over the firing of an inept personnel director. He searched for signs of health care needs in the face and the gait of every employee he passed, and he pushed for more equipment in the tiny exercise room, despite the lack of funds. And in May he watched the interchangeable automatons advance to replace their faulty brethren.

VANILLA TUNA

September

"So you can be the Monday/Tuesday person and I'll be the Wednesday/Thursday person."

"And Friday?"

"I figured Fridays we'd be on our own … a day to maybe slip out and run errands, make an appointment … without putting out the other person. Of course the schedule could be changed any time, at our mutual agreement, of course. We'll start October first."

"And we should always be punctual."

"Absolutely. I'll be at your house at 7:25 on the dot every morning, whether to pick you up because I'm driving or to jump into your car because you're driving."

"And in the winter I'll have the car running so you don't need to move from your warm car to my freezing car."

"That would be nice."

"You don't have a problem leaving your car in my drive-way all day?"

"Do you live in a bad neighborhood?"

"No ..."

"Dicey neighbors to worry about?"

"No ..."

"Then I have no worries. Doors will be locked. I keep no valuables."

"Should we have penalties for, say, being late, making the other person wait?"

"We won't be late."

"Deal."

"Deal."

October

"Glad I'm on time this morning. I know this sounds weird but the clock in my shower shows it's six."

"Who has a clock in the shower?"

"It's connected to a mirror, but it's dropped off the wall so many times that the clock doesn't function properly anymore. It just says six."

"When did this start?"

"Last month."

"You mean like it's 7:27 A.M. here in the car, so all the time your clock reads six o'clock?"

"No, just the numeral six. Digital thing."

"A single number? No clock time? Clock time should show several numbers, like seven twenty-seven has three."

"Right, plus a colon in the digital world. But I've only got the numeral six. A single six."

"And no colon."

"Nope, I don't merit a colon."

"And what do you make of this?"

"I figure its import will reveal itself over time."

"In the shower?"

"In the shower."

"In the shower things are washed away, become new. At least six is a spiritually positive number."

"How's that?"

"Six is the human number. Man was created on the sixth day."

"Well, my man was asleep this morning. It would have been helpful to know the time in the shower. Keep me on track. I lay my clothes out every night, for instance. Got to be organized."

"So do I. I can't think straight in the morning. I can't do anything without coffee."

"I need milk."

"Is coffee okay in the car? Your car I mean."

"Sure, got these handy cup holder holes right here."

"I wouldn't want to create a mess … like pretzels aren't a good idea."

"Funny how people drink coffee in the car but not milk. And pretzels, they're out."

"And I can't work at night, on school work, I mean."

"Me either. Sometimes I'll bring a stack of grading home just for show, but I never do it."

"I do the same thing. I'll pick up something and stuff it in my bag especially if Krandall is still in her office and watching. I figure it gives that eagle eye of hers something to fix on."

"King Krandall, she may sign my paycheck but she sucks the life out of me."

"Do you know she used to grade our lesson plans? That was before you arrived."

"*Grade* them?"

"Every week. I used to earn just a C, and I'm great in the classroom, very effective. I wanted to throttle her."

"Can't say I'm anymore fond of her myself. When I first got here I nearly quit on the spot because she told me how she could deny my health insurance based on my performance. I thought *How the hell do you think you can do that legally, bitch?*, but I needed the job. In retaliation I took a sick day and went shopping the next week."

"True confessions time I guess."

"What is it people say after being in Vegas? What happens in Vegas stays in Vegas."

"So what happens in the car pool stays in the car pool."

"Deal."

"Deal."

November

"Tonight, rather today, it's our anniversary."

"Oh! How many years?"

"Twenty-five."

"Congratulations!"

"Well, congratulations is actually sort of a weird response."

"But twenty-five years ..."

"Wish me a *happy* anniversary instead. Congratulations sounds like we've finished some great effort."

"I never thought of it that way."

"And I don't want it to be over."

"That's lovely. How's the number in the shower?"

"Still stuck at six."

"If the number goes down to five, that's grace. If the clock elevates to the number seven, spiritual perfection."

"I can't imagine any perfection on my part ... grace either. Thanks for warming up the car this morning though."

"No problem."

December

"We're at the number four in the shower."

"From six to four. Four is positive. Maybe it's a Christmas gift. You've progressed."

"Maybe it's a countdown. I must be a slow learner. It took two months to turn to a new number on the clock and I've gone backwards."

"Spirtually the number four means you're grounded."

"But I jumped a number. Seems I'm regressing. I skipped five, that grace thing, like I told you. At this rate I won't get anywhere for another two months. I don't even know why we're discussing this number business."

"The number four means creativity, but creativity in a terrestrial way. That's where the grounding comes."

"I don't feel creative. What's a negative number?"

"Eleven ... eleven denotes disorder."

"That's me, an eleven. Long ago I was hired on the eleventh of August and even longer ago I was born on the eleventh of October."

"Well I'm obviously getting somewhere. Krandall smiled at me yesterday. Told me I was doing a good job and actually touched my shoulder. I didn't even get a horrifying burn mark from the hell fire in her fingers. I checked once I got home. Figured I'd have to take advantage of that health insurance if she'd made a permanent mark."

January

"I want to make a tuna casserole for them, you know, because they'll be home late after the visitation and they'll have all those out-of-town family members to feed."

"But we won't be to your house until 5:30 tonight and we've got to meet at the funeral home at 6:15."

"I can do it."

"Okay. Seems tight to me."

"I'm the one in the kitchen. I'll judge the time. But listen, let me ask your opinion, cooking-wise, I mean. I don't have any cream of mushroom soup."

"But that's key! It's the smoothing agent. My mother always made tuna noodle casserole with cream of mushroom soup."

"So did mine, but I'm thinking of just using some broth."

"Yeah, maybe to start with, but you need the creaminess."

"I've got a soy ... a vanilla soy milk."

"*Vanilla* tuna?"

"Or I think I may have some sour cream. How about if I stir sour cream into the broth?"

"That sounds pretty repulsive as well. They don't mix."

"Maybe they don't mix for you."

"They don't mix for anyone. I'd never eat it."

"I don't recall asking you to eat it."

"Well, maybe I'll just go to the store tonight and make the stuff tomorrow."

"That would be better. You've got to work with compatible ingredients."

February

"Geez, *pleeease* remember to warm the car in the morning."

"Sorry. Doesn't feel so cold to me."

"Well, it is. And the shower clock jumped to two."

"No three?"

"No three."

"Maybe this erratic jumping, it's trying to tell you something."

"No, you tell me what it's telling me. You're the numberology person."

"*Nu*-merology."

"Same thing."

"Not really."

"So tell me."

"I can't remember."

"Yes you can. Go ahead. You don't want to tell me, do you?"

"Three means completeness. That's what you've skipped."

"Completeness ... Is that a word? And are you implying I'm missing fulfillment in my life? I'm the one who's married, remember?"

"Two means difference. The world's off kilter. Something's missing."

"I'll say. And what if the clock turns to zero?"

"Zero doesn't exist on a clock."

"But what if it did?"

"Zero is a vanishing. It's so elusive that no one even knows who invented the concept of zero, though there are many theories."

"Spare me."

"It's just an empty place, a place holder. It's completely without value."

March

"Okay, I'm trying to understand. How come she asked you to chair this outside committee and not me? And who forgot to warm up the car again?"

"We'd spoken about it a couple of weeks ago."

"Without me?"

"I don't need to involve you in everything I do on school grounds. I'm my own person."

"But what about the car pool?"

"What about the car pool? The car pool is the car pool and school ... our positions ... are separate things."

"And I'll bet you've earned a raise for this."

"Yes, a small one."

"But we could have done it together."

"Could we? I'm beginning to doubt that."

"And we could have shared the small raise."

"Is that all you're thinking about? It's simply not in my purview to give you my hard-earned money."

"I see. A lot like it's not in my gastronomic purview to be eating vanilla tuna."

"Can't you let anything go? I didn't make it with vanilla, and I didn't make it for you anyway. Based on your recommendation, *your* recommendation because I listen to people and consider their opinions, I made regular old tuna casserole with the three main ingredients: elbow noodles, tuna chunks, and the goddamn *CREAM* of mushroom soup. The three heavenly ingredients, three, the number meaning completeness, if you remember, the word you didn't like. And the family really liked it. And they told me so. And I got a lot of satisfaction, which I'm not feeling at the moment sitting here."

"Completeness still isn't a word."

April

"You've got to stop slamming on the brakes for the butterflies."

"But I don't want them to land in the grill. I can't kill them, all that beauty."

"They're just butterflies."

"*Just* butterflies?"

"Plus, think scientifically ... or maybe mathematically ... you can't judge the speed and velocity of the common yellow butterfly as compared to the half-ton road vehicle."

"Maybe I could if I drove like you, always speeding. Hmm, how might one judge the velocity of the potential police car behind us ... ."

"I don't speed. I keep it to eight miles over the speed limit. No one is going to stop me for that."

"Okay, you use that logic when the time comes."

"Speeding, *official* speeding, starts at ten miles over the speed limit."

"Right, who told you that?"

"Let's keep in mind I've never *had* to use that logic because we've *never been stopped* when I've been driving. And if I remember right the other person in this car *was* stopped not long ago."

"That wasn't for speeding."

"Still broke the law, not moving into the left-hand lane when the cop had that car stopped on the right-hand shoulder."

"But it was dismissed. Even the state admitted they'd just put that law into effect without any citizens' warning."

"Still sent you to court, sweet pea."

"This is a ridiculous conversation."

May

"How's the clock?"

"Stuck at two."

"Two is—"

"Don't remind me."

June

"You just hit the brakes to avoid that bird."

"No I didn't."

"Yes, you did. And you give me grief about slowing for the butterflies."

"*Slowing?*" You slam on the brakes and I'm not ready. Do you know what it's like not to be in control when you do that? Think about me in the passenger seat."

"That's what happens when you're a control *freak*."

"At least my vehicle is clean."

"And mine isn't?"

"You might clean it up Sunday evenings before we drive for the week."

"I can't help it if I haul around donated articles for Gently Used To You. You should try doing a good turn for others sometime. Are you even involved in a charity?"

"I write my checks … plus, must be a bunch of junk you're hauling around if it leaves such a mess in the car. And why do you have to use my seat for that debris?"

"*Your* seat? This is *my* car."

"Yes, but you make the space available to me, as I do for you in my *clean* vehicle."

July

"I'm afraid spiritually I need to return to the numeral one."

"What's that supposed to mean?"

"… The committee is becoming too labor intensive."

"Is this the excuse you've come up with?"

"The number one, spiritually it means unity and commencement. It's time for me to move on, to start anew."

"So, we're finally at zero, place holders without value."

"You might check your clock."

"Your car is too cold anyway."

ALBATROSS

She had just thrown her bath towel, yet again, into the winding and unwinding dryer tumbler kept in the rain forest. At least that's what Ben had called it—when he had been there. This place, the place he had referred to as the rain forest, was really the kitchen of their rented apartment in Christchurch where the small dryer tucked under the lone window did not vent through the outside wall, as would have been required in the States. Instead, the moisture was pumped back into the kitchen through a round vent the size of a luncheon plate at the bottom right-hand corner of the appliance. Hillary sat at the small breakfast table, multiple air bubbles popping up under the surface of its covering, a thick but cheap paper meant to look like real wood grain. She eyed the dripping green walls.

She and Ben had left Auckland on New Zealand's North Island to spend July's winter school holiday on the South Island in Christchurch, but Ben was also entertaining the idea of a teaching position at Christchurch's University of Canterbury. He was full of himself. They'd only spent a semester in

Auckland and already he was thinking of leaving for another New Zealand university.

"You can't just flit about like that," warned Hillary while Ben had planned the Christchurch trip. "Think of the stereotype of the ugly American."

"Remember what David told us?" Ben had reminded her. David had been their New Zealand contact at the University of Auckland before arriving. "He said, 'You're golden to land a position.' *Golden*. He said New Zealand needs academics because the younger generation goes off to seek the rest of the world."

"I remember what David said, but it's gone to your head."

"I can do whatever I want."

"No one can do whatever they want, Ben."

She hadn't wanted to move, even temporarily, to Auckland at all. She had avoided discussions of the possibility in the months before they had left the States, hoping Ben would drop the idea, but he had instead interpreted her silence as a confirmation of his decision. To add to Hillary's worries, they had left their modest home in Richmond, Virginia, in the hands of dubious renters after a hastily arranged deal Tidewater University had set up with Ben allowing the school to host a pair of incoming academics.

"We don't even know who they are," complained Hillary. "We've never had kids in the house. I'd rather meet them all first."

"And *then* tell them no once they're here? The school knows them. It'll be all right."

"Where are they even from?"

"Does it make a difference?"

"No, not really, because I don't want anyone in the house, Ben."

"And the mortgage will be paid ... how?"

.   .   .

Most of all Hillary missed her enormous gardens behind their house and her small business selling flower arrangements. Over the past few months in Auckland, as winter had come to the Pacific, Hillary's mind had fled to her Virginia flower beds awakening to spring—bulbs pushing, rhizomes spreading, roots digging, and finally the blooms. The blooms. But there her picture distorted as she imagined small booted feet smashing down her Star Gazer lilies with their delicate stems, tiny curious hands snaking themselves through her Shasta daisies, and faded orange and yellow bouncing balls landing within her clumps of evenly spaced Bressingham blue hosta. Short compact bodies would crash together in play and rip her top heavy peonies, and some dog could—*Christ, what if they had a dog? They'd forgotten to refuse dogs in the rental agreement*—well, a dog could just wreak absolute havoc.

"For God's sakes—"

Ben was always saying God's *sakes*. How many sakes were there?

"You only work with flowers," Ben had urged when trying to convince her of the move. He had meant the line as a positive suggestion, a new way of thinking, but Ben never seemed to realize how his words came across to other people. "I don't know why you can't just leave."

I don't know why you can't... . Hillary wondered if Ben ever wondered what she *could*.

"And what's wrong with a flower shop? My sister *owns* one. Remember also that she buys half my flowers. She'll have to find a new source for a year. And when we return I can't see how she'll easily drop that relationship. And where will that leave us?"

"She loves you."

This was no answer and Hillary knew Ben had already inked the housing deal with Tidewater without consulting her.

•   •   •

"I'm thinking of going back to Auckland," announced Ben just a week after their holiday began in Christchurch.

I. Again *I.*

"But we just got here."

"This place is too dismal anyway," Ben continued. "The rooms are either too wet or too cold. I've got a rain forest for a kitchen and then I move to winter in the bedroom and Antarctica in the front room." He put his hand theatrically to his forehead in a mock salute and leaned forward, as if in search of something down the apartment's long hallway. "I'm on the lookout for Commodore Perry in there. *Four* degrees. I'm *freezing.* I can't ..."

I, I, I.

Hillary wondered whether Ben was being sarcastic in a Fahrenheit sense with his claim of temperature, or whether he meant four degrees Celsius, which was actually more like forty degrees Fahrenheit. But he was right, the house was far too cold. They kept all the rooms' doors closed to conserve heat. Since landing in Auckland, Hillary had urged Ben to do the temperature conversions, to learn the new system, but Ben could not let go of American ways. He found New Zealand's shower heads set too low and the country's architecture too modern. Moreover, ridiculously affecting what he thought was a New Zealand accent, Ben was constantly being asked by New Zealanders to repeat himself, adding to his general annoyance.

"That heated mattress cover is the only thing that gets me through the night. I wake up and my nose is freezing and my shoulders are like ice. You know how I am. From the shoulders up I feel like some solid Greek stone bust, like that part of my body could be chipped at, lifted off, and put on display." He hunched his shoulders and stood still. "I'm the A-maaa-zing Frozen Man."

Ben had always had popsicle toes and, except during the warmest months of summer, wore socks to bed even in the States.

"You could wear a scarf," Hillary offered, enjoying the cartoonish image.

Ben ignored her. "And that front room. God, it's got to be in the twenties when we wake up. Feels like we should be out-doors but we're *inside*. You won't run the space heater."

"Well, it seems a bit silly to be running the heat at night when we're not using the room."

Ben overlooked his wife's rationale. "Plus, with the ten-foot-high ceilings, I feel like even when we are in the room, we're heating the ceiling rather than where we're standing. We're heating the up there rather than the down here. This place is just one long unheated hallway with multiple door choices. It's like a game show," he said sarcastically. "You get your choice of room, in order of chill."

On the day Hillary and Ben had arrived in Christchurch, *The Press* had run a story titled "Our Cult of Cold," asking "Why are New Zealand houses so cold and why do New Zea-landers put up with it?" The story pointed out how the country had just endured its coldest June since 1972.

"Hooray to be here in July instead," Ben had moaned.

Their rental house in Auckland, leased for a year, sported the depthless straight lines and boxy architecture typical of New Zealand's modern homes. The interior may have blazed white, the rooms sparsely furnished with that which belonged in American office buildings, but it was warm. In contrast, the home they had rented for their time here on the South Island had been built in 1892 as two divided townhouses, mirror im-ages of one another. The owners lived on one side, top and bottom, and rented out two individual apartments next door. The leased areas were called "serviced apartments," but could be taken as Bed and Breakfast accommodations if desired. Ben and Hillary had rented the place as what was also called a "self-contained" apartment and were expected to use the kitchen as they liked. Certainly the holiday would be cheaper that way, but also less romantic.

Ben griped daily about the lack of heat, starting from his entrance through the front door, and he continued his complaints while traipsing down the first floor hallway toward the flight of stairs leading to the second floor, where their apartment really began. Because of the unusually cold weather, the place had not proved homey at all. At the small landing at the top of the long staircase, straight ahead stood a closed wooden door leading to the kitchen. Looking directly left, the next wooden door, when opened, led to the bathroom. Turning a bit more to the left, and in the middle of the long upper hallway, stood another closed door to the main bedroom. At the hallway's end, there were yet two more doors, both shut, one to the front room and next to it a second leading to a miniscule second bedroom which, at the moment, balanced the couple's three suitcases, one on top of the other, upon a spartan single bed. The owners had not even placed a pillow at one end, as though it might take up too much space. In all there were five identical doors along the hallway. And all were closed to keep the heat in—what heat there was. Moreover, to open a door meant letting out whatever prior heat might have been generated within the room. And with a lack of transoms, the apartment's interior was like that of a dark icebox. To open the doors required sunlight, and Christchurch had not seen a ray since Hillary and Ben's arrival.

In a weak effort to combat the cold, in the middle of each room sat a one-foot-wide by some two-foot-tall electric radiator, but even the one in the bedroom, which Hillary kept on high twenty-four hours a day, lacked the oomph to warm the bedroom's interior above sixty degrees Fahrenheit—or, to make Ben feel even colder, fifteen Celsius. Hillary liked to do the conversions.

The bathroom off the bedroom remained permanently cold, the bedroom radiator's heat never seeming to seep around the corner. "Radiant heat" obviously did not mean moving heat. And without the benefit of a venting fan or the ability, or desire, to open a window—Who would want to let in the frosty air?—what was put into the stagnant chilled air of the bathroom stayed there: humidity created from the running of two hot showers and all human smells. The towels stayed damp and the environment dank. Hillary had found no cleaning supplies below the bathroom's small sink save a half-used can of Glade's Essence of Vanilla, promising *NO MESS* when sprayed; yet it had been tucked into the lower left-hand corner of the cupboard as though hiding, unable to admit it would add yet another lingering odor into the inert air space.

The front room stayed the coldest because they chose to use it—Ben would claim that Hilary chose to use it—only to watch a bit of television in the evening, before the cold sent them shivering to their heated bed to read. With an enormous and lovely nineteenth-century bay window looking north, but without any appearance of the sun, the room had never had a chance to warm up naturally during their stay. In the mornings this room won the cold race, coming in at forty-eight or forty-nine. (*Nine C!*)

She found herself resorting to useful deception where Ben was concerned, having hidden the small gauge displaying both Fahrenheit and Celsius when Ben had asked the temperature. He didn't need to know. Earlier that week she had also hidden the fact that she had accidentally left the door to the kitchen freezer slightly ajar the previous night, turning the ice cream they'd bought at PAK'n SAVE to a creamy white soup—and certainly not helping the kitchen radiator's fight to raise the temperature.

Ice flakes the size of quarters had formed.

"And we're even harboring enormous ice crystals *in here*," Ben had concluded the following afternoon, surveying the freezer's interior walls just an hour or two after Hillary had discovered her mistake and shut the door properly.

"Must just be their refrigeration," she had mumbled.

"The ice cream's or mine?" Ben had asked grimly.

．　　．　　．

Part of staying in the apartment was learning its quirks and how to heat its corners—and not expecting too much. The bright spot was the kitchen, not because of its access to light, but because it warmed more easily. It was small, perhaps six by seven feet, and the ceiling hung lower than in the other rooms. Hillary soon discovered how to set about her morning kitchen work in steps. As soon as she entered through the door (and closed it), she turned the electric radiator on as high as she could. There was really no point though because after filling the electric water kettle with water—for some reason no one in New Zealand ever heated water on the stovetop's burners, or the hobs as they were called—she had to turn off the radiator in order to plug the kettle in. Four plugs hung in a row two feet above the counter, but to run the electric kettle and the electric radiator simultaneously overloaded the circuit. The kettle worked its boiling magic in a flash, however, in less than a minute it seemed—would that the room heat worked this way—and she was then able to unplug the kettle and quickly turn the heat back on.

Each socket first required the flipping of a switch at the wall, the turning on of the electricity, an odd step by American standards. Hillary had often wondered whether electricity would leak from the socket if the switch remained in the on position after she left the kitchen. She imagined electricity dribbling, Dali-like, down the wall in her absence.

The dryer and microwave also balked at being run simultaneously and simply snapped off in protest. All of the kitchen's larger appliances stood clumped together on the far wall of the room next to its only window. A small dryer sat under the window and the microwave, obscuring the window's lower right-hand corner, was propped on its flat top surface. A refrigerator, some eighteen inches wide by two and half feet tall, sat atop a freezer of the same size. Standing in front of the refrigerator and freezer, Hillary was still taller than the two stacked appliances. To her right and tucked into the corner sat the washing machine. In this corner of the kitchen dimness prevailed, especially since the refrigerator/freezer combination blocked out any light coming from the window just four feet away. When retrieving clothes from a load of wash, Hilary's head blocked out the rest of the light emanating from the ceiling fixture above. She felt as though she were sinking her right arm into a black hole. In addition, the machine offered cold wash only and Hillary wondered just how clean she was getting the clothes.

Because of the winter weather and the lack of a venting fan, the bathroom towels never dried completely before the next shower, so she ran the dryer a good deal. But the dryer, venting into the kitchen, created Ben's so-called rain forest, which, of course, then created more humidity the house was incapable of disposing of. It was a vicious circle that would continue to promote the unhealthy mold Americans were so aware of but which New Zealanders overlooked and accepted.

The article in *The Press* had noted how New Zealanders dealt with the cold by claiming it was good for them rather than doing anything about it like installing necessary wall insulation and, as they were called here, double-glazed windows. Yet, talk to a New Zealander and he or she would moan just as much as a foreigner could about the cold. "We pretend it's not cold," they would all admit in one form or another, but the urgent call made to citizens by some in the press and the government to change their views toward housing had not yet been heard—or heeded. "It's not that cold there," a friend from the U.S. had emailed after checking New Zealand's weather and doing the Celsius to Fahrenheit conversion. Hillary had written back, correcting him, "It's in the low 40s during the day, but I don't come in to find refuge in a cheerfully warm house, leaving the gloom behind. The same penetrating cold is in the house as well."

She felt like complaining so she continued. "The uninsulated walls are pulsing with chill within the room. No sun comes through the window, and the drapes are actually drawn—somewhat uselessly—to hold back the cold seeping through the single-pane windows."

"Come home then," suggested her friend.

Hillary composed a brief and vague response: "I don't like to fly." And then she turned the computer off.

·   ·   ·

"We can make the best of it," Hillary assured Ben with as much cheer as she could muster following his comment concerning his own personal refrigeration, but she knew their mood together depended, as it always did, on Ben's outlook. She hoped the New Zealanders' friendliness and her husband's scouting around the University of Canterbury would quiet his agitation.

But it hadn't. And he was leaving.

"And me?" she asked.

"I've left that up to you. We've paid for this place, and I don't want to take away from your holiday."

"My holiday *alone?*" Hillary practically sneered. Her eyes narrowed. "Just what do you want to get back to in Auckland, Ben?"

·   ·   ·

Hillary watched the unwinding dryer toss her single towel. After tumbling one way for a period of time, the dryer stopped completely, seeming to contemplate its progress, and then reversed its tumbling direction after some five seconds, continuing on with its job. Hillary felt like the dryer's tumbler herself, pulled a little bit this way, pulled a little bit that way, all the while ending up in the same place. She tried to think "No worries," as people said here, but she did have worries. Ben had left.

She moved to the front room. The weather was finally "fine," as New Zealanders said, meaning real rays of sunshine were pushing through the bay window's glass in the front room late that morning. *Ben never stuck around to feel this.* The room's temperature had risen to almost seventy degrees—*nineteen!* Hillary sat down to read *The Press* at the round table placed in the window's half moon curve. She swung her knees above the table's edge and placed her bare feet on the table's surface to absorb the heat of the sun. *The Press* was unwieldy, as most New Zealand newspapers were, too wide to be read in bed lying down or next to someone sitting close. Trying to fold an individual section back on top of itself felt like an attempt at catching waves of water.

The paper had reviewed a theater production currently playing in Wellington, on the southern tip of the North Island, called *Puppetry of the Penis*, a show promising full frontal male nudity. Repulsed by the title, Hillary still continued to read. Several of Wellington's citizens had shown up to audition, the story said, something the producers apparently encouraged, but their "limp offerings" had not measured up to show standards. Hillary lay the paper down. *This* is morning reading? She felt prudish. Despite the sun and "fine" weather outside, the weather in Hillary's own world did not feel fine.

She turned to the Classifieds and tried to laugh at the ads for escorts: "Paris petite" read one and another offered a "horny fallen angel." Several escorts, in fact, claimed to be angels of some sort and all promised to be discreet. A customer's requests could run from "vanilla to bizarre" offered one, and another professed to be "rude as you like." Potential customers could choose to go to a dungeon, a steam sauna maze, or a place of "slick sinful heat." One ad simply requested, "If you're a boob man ring me," and Classy Cindy's "headlights were always on hi." Most intriguingly, someone professing to be new to town described herself as having "voluptuous understanding." Hillary recognized the comma's absence between the two descriptives but still mused over how understanding could be voluptuous. The lack of punctuation made the phrase seem somehow so rich. Someone at the airport offered "toys to spice you up," nude massages were popular all around, and one Chinese woman simply claimed to be "nice to hold." Hillary had no doubt.

She wondered what—or who—Ben had returned to in Auckland. Was he receiving voluptuous understanding?

She was trying to make do, trying to make a holiday for herself. After Ben left, Hillary had called the owners and switched her stay's designation from "serviced apartment" to "bed and breakfast." Doing so meant gazing at a long list of breakfast choices each evening and circling requests for the following day. She looked forward to a few sumptuous morning meals, but after one day she cancelled the request. The owners had been nearly nonplussed at the reversal, especially the woman who labored over her stove and took great pride in the results. But how could she explain that since Ben's departure she had been swimming in the bedroom's lavender bed. Even the heated mattress cover had not comforted her. The dining table where she sat here in the front room was now surrounded by four looming large wooden chairs. Previously half the table's surface and two of the chairs had been covered with Ben's academic papers and folders. Now they lay bare, and she felt tiny and alone when first the woman, with her broad smile, and then her husband arrived—it took two people to bring in both trays—with a breakfast far too grand for one person—muesli, orange juice, toast, jams, honey, butter, black currant tea, milk, sugar, a plate of steaming eggs and baked tomatoes, fruit muffins, and napkin-wrapped silverware. Besides the breakfast, the couple had brought her the copy of *The Press*, and each tray had been decorated with fresh flowers. Hillary knew she was being pitied.

During the day she had felt spied on as well. New Zealand women, young and old, businesswomen and housewives alike, tended to wear black, and Hillary sported a powder blue winter jacket. Everyone here, male and female alike, ignored the cold whereas during her stay with Ben in Christchurch, Hillary had worn layers of fleece which she donned like a practiced rhythm the moment she awoke. Then, quickly heating up, she walked around smelling like the morning's cooking grease she had used.

On this particular day, despite having been fed the sumptuous meal instead, she still swore she smelled of oil beneath her conspicuous power blue jacket.

She felt noticed, even flagrant. In front of the Canterbury Museum, conducting a survey for their class, the young school girls in their below-the-knee, dark blue and green kilts fell upon her—*a foreigner!*— and an old man stared at her as she asked the produce man at the New World grocery about carrots. "*Carrots*," the man mouthed once the employee had turned back to his rows of stacked peppers. She thought him daft. "I knew from your pronunciation you had to be American," he then said in a pleasant voice. "Here on holiday or are you retired?" *Retired?* Hillary couldn't imagine being retired at her age. How old did she look?

Just alone she wanted to tell the man, but instead she merely mentioned how much better New Zealand's carrots were than those in the United States and left.

Today here at the table in the sun she resolved to leave Christchurch for somewhere where she wouldn't be so obviously out of place. An ad offering tours to Akaroa, a touristy town of just 650 inhabitants on nearby Banks Peninsula, caught her eye in the paper. In Akaroa she could be just another tourist. She had no desire, however, to sit on a bus, or even a small van, with a swarm of people who would find it important to ask where she was from. She leaned to her left and picked up the phonebook from a side table, opening to the letter R, and used her index finger to scan for rental car ads.

.   .   .

The roads to Akaroa offer spectacular scenery, but also some of the most challenging winding roads one might ever encounter. After consulting her Lonely Planet guide of New Zealand, Hillary chose to take what was referred to as the easier way, State Highway 75, rather than the route described by the writers as "sometimes treacherous." The editors called Akaroa "a delight," having retained its French roots. Captain Cook, believing what he saw to be an island, had come up the waters within the peninsula in 1770, naming the area for his botanist Sir Joseph Banks. In Maori, the language of New Zealand's indigenous peoples, Akaroa meant Long Harbor—or Long Harbour by New Zealand's spelling.

At first Hillary had been charmed during her drive, enjoying the roadside warnings about sliding WHEN FROSTY and finding that, curiously, every drain culvert along the way had been named. Signs admonished citizens *Don't be a tosser*, a gas station was a *bowser*, and the radio news advised of a *smash* on a nearby bridge. On the talk show she had tuned into, the host urged listeners to get "a new jab a year" against the flu and finished each provocative topic's discussion with "Whaddya reckon? Whaddya reckon?"

But after eighty-two kilometers—she no longer cared about the conversion—through mountain villages, or really just the individual portals to mountain villages—Motukarara and Little River, offering the only store along the way as well as, surprisingly, a first aid station, followed by Cooptown and Hilltop and Duvauchelle and Robinson's Bay and Takamatua—a route comprised of what soon became monotonous loops and severe inclines amidst endless glorious landscape, Hillary had had enough … enough beauty … enough landscape … and longed to arrive at her destination. She was, after all, driving on the other side of the road and, due to the curves, constantly yanking on the steering wheel and down shifting. She started to believe that her trip to Akaroa was more arduous than Cook's could have been two and a half centuries before.

Parking at last on narrow rue Lavaud had proved easy and once out of the car she marched half a block further up the street right into the small Akaroa Museum. She'd get a little culture under her belt, forget her troubles, and start understanding the European/Maori culture clash. She could return to

Auckland ... before returning to the States perhaps ... with more to talk about than Ben.

The woman in charge at the museum's main desk welcomed her customer with a broad smile. Seeing that Hillary was counting out the $4NZ (less than $3US) for a self-guided tour of the museum, the woman snapped her cash drawer open and responded cheerily, "Fantastic!" as though this were one of her most exhilarating exchanges with a customer to date. The woman seemed to be glowing, radiating like the sun, and Hillary didn't feel even remotely ... yellow. She felt brown, mouse brown.

Fantastic! and *Brilliant!* were overused in New Zealand, at least by American standards. One might as well walk around Iowa bursting forth with overwrought and hyperbolic terms like *Tremendous!* and *Fantabulous!* at every chance. My handing you a $4 entrance fee is really not *Fantastic!* thought Hillary. It's actually quite ordinary, required—necessary really. If I have $4 I get in. If I give you $3 or $2 ... or $1 and a steaming mug of tea, I don't. Then again, she had to admit the response *Great!* had become equally trite in America. How was it any different? Setting up a mutual time to meet for lunch in the States was not *Great!* Such a word should have implied, "That's wonderful! I can *hardly believe* this lunch meeting is going to happen!" Instead it just meant a generic, "That works; see you then." In an earlier generation the outdated *Super!* had been the superlative of choice. In her mood, Hillary was happy to note its demise.

She exhausted the museum quickly and an hour later Hillary stared at a menu at a local pub's restaurant. During their months in New Zealand, she had always enjoyed pointing out to Ben the semantic differences in English usage. Here an appetizer was an entrée and an entrée was a main. One ordered either a half pint or a handle or a jug of beer rather than a glass or a mug or a pitcher. Raisins were sultanas, zucchini were courgettes, sweet potatoes were kumara, and green pepper was capsicum. Today, however, she felt stumped when reading the restaurant choices. But she soon found the restaurant's single employee full of explanations and ready to serve her any late meal she liked.

New Zealanders kept up with your conversation with a barrage of "yeahs." After landing in Auckland, Hillary at first thought she was saying too much to people, insulting their intelligence. But now, as she asked her culinary questions at the bar, she already anticipated the *yeah* to follow nearly every clause. She no longer felt she and her conversant were talking over one another. *Yeah*s were, in fact, multi-talented, used to punctuate a sentence, indicate listening, or take the place of a silence. They had no equivalent in the English language. She counted out her dollars and change slowly, for in New Zealand one always paid for food and drink directly after ordering, and the woman at the bar waited patiently through Hillary's simple math process. Hillary looked forward to her salad smothered in feta. Every food that could handle it in New Zealand contained feta.

The drive home felt quite fine this time. Hillary whipped the car around each curve, hugging the mountainside, and threw in a couple of tentative *yeah*s into the conversation when she stopped at the lone store along the way in Little River for something to drink. She liked that no one said, "Excuse me?" when she spoke. Ben would have been envious.

Afterward, back in Christchurch, she had to admit that she felt quite a bit better. Than what, she wasn't quite ready to analyze.

.   .   .

That weekend she extended her stay another week, pleasing her hosts next door, but within two days she still itched to remove herself from the old home's confines. Her decision to make the seven-hour trip south to Dunedin proved as spontaneous as the decision to drive to Akaroa the week prior. Hillary would explore another peninsula, something else that stuck out—more than she did. The tip of the remote Otago Peninsula was home to The Royal Albatross Centre at the Taiaroa Head Nature Reserve, the only mainland colony for giant royal albatrosses in the world. Visitors would be too busy eyeing the nesting fledglings to be interested in her.

Since she had prepaid the apartment's rent, she didn't tell the owners next door that she was temporarily leaving. Why should she? She didn't have to.

She didn't call Ben either.

But he hadn't called her.

·   ·   ·

The drive to Dunedin was swift, keeping her on a two-lane highway until entering the isolated Otagao Peninsula. The narrow shoreline crept too close to the road for Hillary's comfort. Plus, once on the road leading away from Dunedin, she hadn't known she would still need to drive so far beyond the city. She felt she was leaving New Zealand altogether. Finally she arrived at the tip of the peninsula, seemingly at the end of the world.

After the conservatory's usual museum visit, quick orientation, and requisite short video, Hillary and a dozen or so other visitors climbed, single file, along a narrow zigzagging path up the steep side of the precipice behind the museum building. At the end of the trail lay their destination, the albatross observatory. The group became quieter and watchful as they neared the area. She thought of the group as guests rather than visitors or tourists, for even though she had paid her ticket price, just as she had done at the Akaoroa Museum, she felt privileged to be allowed to walk within the protected reserve. Their guide had warned the group that at this time of year they would be highly unlikely to see any adult albatross swoop in to feed its young, both parents being far out to sea. The season was too advanced. Adult albatrosses had arrived the previous September, mated in October, laid eggs in November, incubating them until mid-January or early February, and then tended and guarded their young for what amounted to three hundred days. Here in July it was too late in the breeding year, the young woman explained, to expect to experience the drama of a feeding parent, especially since the fledglings themselves would be gone in just a few weeks, sometime in September. The only thing keeping them down at this point was their weight. They were actually too heavy to fly. Protectively, Nature had caused their parents to overfeed them.

Most of the "tour" occurred in the observatory, but that was all right with Hillary. The structure itself was just a shell, a small, squat square of a building containing nothing in its interior save a few explanatory diagrams—which everyone would ignore, wanting to see the real albatrosses instead—and low benches along the windowed walls next to which hung binoculars held by curly black cords. Out the window the individual nests dotted what looked like a vast rocky field. At first Hillary could hardly detect the nests since they blended in with the landscape. They were neither as numerous, nor as close as Hillary had expected. *You're not in a zoo.* Only experienced employees could walk through the area, and even then just a couple at a time. Hillary felt as though she were looking across the craggy moors of Scotland, though the peninsula ended in a dizzingly high cliff, violent waves crashing far below.

The guide was silent as she knew her visitors needed to absorb the site. She listened to them speak in low tones while politely sharing binoculars, family members pointing where other family members should look. Soon this pointing would extend to those around them as people became more comfortable, curious, and aware of what they were seeing.

Despite the birds' distance from the observatory, one didn't have to use the binoculars to see the young nesting albatrosses; in fact, viewing them without the aid of binoculars took away some of the sadness in seeing them at first. Each nest held just one fledgling, a fluffy, brownish, somewhat mottled bird—a striking contrast to its mostly white parents—constantly bracing against the fierce and unrelenting wind. Solitary in their nests, each seemed unconcerned, however, with the harsh conditions or the lack of social or physical contact, the next nest being some one hundred yards away. The birds could not yet fly, though they now and then rose slightly from the nest, almost standing in anticipation, to test their wings in mock flight. The tearing wind did not cow them; instead, it seemed to give them encouragement. Hillary was surprised at the fledglings' size, as large as their parents, even larger. The birds appeared clumsy when not leaning into the wind. They were practically adults, yet simply did not grasp their capabilities.

A small boy's voice broke the reverenced silence the guide had allowed to descend on the visitors. "Won't they fall off the cliff?"

Hillary could not see the boy, but as annoyed as she was with his interruption, she was curious to know the answer to the question.

"I'm afraid some ten percent of the fledglings will fall below into the water to be eaten by sharks." The visitors all recoiled inwardly at this thought, though the guide had offered the statistic without any tone of lament.

Because of the boy's question, the guide took the opportunity to say more about the life of an albatross. "Despite the look of desolation before you, the albatross parent really is a devoted one. They constantly fuss over the newly hatched chicks." No one in the observatory looked at her. All eyes were on the nesting fledglings as she spoke. She was used to speaking to the back of people's heads. "Parents share incubation duties for eleven weeks. That's longer than the incubation period of almost any other bird. Each parent will sit on a nest for some two to eight days while its mate is out to sea." She let a note of sarcasm enter her voice. "You'd get tired being out there at sea for days on end, don't you think?" She looked at the boy who had asked the question who nodded, listening and reacting to her as he did his teacher in school. "So on top of that nest, what does the parent do?" She hesitated for the sake of impact, awaiting a guess, perhaps, from someone in the group.

"*Sle-e-ep*," a voice ventured.

A ripple of laughter united the visitors.

"Yes, that's what we would do as humans, but right now the parents have already left for their year at sea." She emphasized the word year.

Someone in the group emitted a low whistle.

"Adult albatrosses only breed every other year," the guide continued.

By now almost everyone in the observatory group had found his or her place, leaning on one knee propped on a bench, shoulder against a particular wall, or balancing comfortably in a corner.

"But don't worry. The young have been in no danger of starving. Throughout their short lives, these albatross fledglings you see have been used to having a parent vanish for weeks. This is all the chicks have known, actually, but their reward for waiting has been a parent returning with a crop full of nutrient-rich food."

The boy spun around. "Is it regurgitated?" he asked excitedly. Grossness always appealed to the young. His mother, standing with one arm around her son's shoulders, appeared slightly embarrassed.

Brilliant. You're absolutely right," affirmed the guide. "A kind of fish oil actually."

Hillary turned from the window toward the young woman. "How can the adults possibly fly so long without becoming exhausted?" she asked. She returned her gaze to the solitary fledglings. "How can they go on and on and be so alone?" she added quietly.

Without any hesitation the guide began again, her voice punctuating through the air of melancholy Hillary's question had left in the room's atmosphere. "It's called dynamic soaring," she explained. "When we think of birds flying, we think of them flapping their wings, and most do, but albatrosses have a special shoulder joint that locks their wings into place. And these wings, as you'll remember from the Visitors Center video, can be up to three meters across. That's some nine and a half feet for those of you who work in feet rather than meters. They can fly incredibly long distances without flapping and travel speeds of up to one hundred and fifteen kilometers."

Here the woman did not offer a number in miles. Hillary was not good with the kilometers-to-miles conversion and simply halved the number in approximation. She would have to look up the mathematical equation on the computer.

"AH!" cried out someone from the group. "Look, *there*!" and then they all saw it, the expansive white underside of a giant adult albatross swooping in over them on a daring angle toward one nest. All in the observatory became paralyzed by the moment of majesty. They forgot the chicks and stared at the single soaring parent, so white against the colorless background. Even their guide was struck with the unexpected scene. The albatross had landed at a nest on what seemed to be the horizon of the cliff, so it remained very far away. Was it feeding the fledgling? Where were the binoculars? While the underside of the albatross is white, the rest of the adult is quite dark. Where did the parent end and the dusky fledgling begin? No time to refocus the lenses properly. It was all happening too quickly. The group of observatory visitors had fallen into a state of disarray.

Hillary only remotely perceived the human furor around her. She had foregone a mad grasp for the nearby binoculars. She already knew what she was seeing in the adult albatross' grand appearance: a lack of deterrence ... deterrence against wind, against Nature, and even against time and space as Hillary knew it in a human sense. She watched the scene feeling a sense of privilege. *So it could happen just like that ... just like that.*

And then just as quickly the albatross parent rose into the air and left. Despite the anxiety generated in most members of the group, each had drunk in the moment given.

Each had seen it. And each had, in his or her own way, felt it.

It could happen just like that.

·   ·   ·

Their guide waited after the extended moment's end to assure her visitors that the adult albatross would not return. When they had quit searching and set their eyes once more on the lonely nesting birds, she began again.

"What you're seeing, these seemingly abandoned fledglings, is Nature telling them that they're grown, ready for more than they think they can take on. When these birds leave, they'll spend the next three to six years over the ocean. They may return to breed here, but they may not."

"How will they know when to leave?" piped up the little boy again in a high voice, not over his excitement at having seen the giant albatross. He had pulled away from his mother.

"They just seem to know," was all the guide could offer, but the answer settled well within the conservatory. Given this encounter with the natural world, the woman's words were enough. "Nature tells them it's all right."

It would happen just like that.

·   ·   ·

Once in Christchurch Hillary threw open the door to her place, *her* place, climbed the stairs to the second floor and walked right to the front room. Though the sun had nearly set, the table for four now welcomed her as a place to collect and organize her thoughts. The newspaper section she'd abandoned, never read, days ago lay open to the current happenings around Christchurch. *Puppet of the Penis* was following her. *That* show! Now it was in the area. "Spot on and straight up," crowed the producers of the Christchurch auditions. "What a show!" This time Hillary smiled.

A pile of the breakfast choice lists lay to one side. Hillary drew up a chair and began circling more items than she could possibly eat the next morning. She then marched back down the stairs to the first floor, exited her front door, and climbed the two steps to her neighbor's small porch. She slid the list of circled breakfast requests into the mail slot. She patted her stomach. She felt sleek, ready to consume.

.   .   .

In Auckland Ben cradled the cell phone in his left hand. The fingers of his right hand moved toward the digits on the upper half of the instrument.

He had made a mistake.

.   .   .

Back at the tip of the Otago Peninsula the first of the albatross fledglings Nature had chosen to lift off the earth was feeling its first real stirrings. It was only the end of July and the fledgling did not know it was to be first, and that being first would still take some weeks, yet it felt stronger somehow. The wind, rather than assaulting the bird, had begun to glide through its feathers.

To look at them, the lone chicks enduring their spare lives on the windy peninsula, an observer could not tell which would cease practicing flight and catch the wind at a new angle, becoming in a moment a bird of flight and graceful promise. But the bird would know.

LOTTIE'S CAVE ROAD

Supposedly Lottie had lived in a nearby cave during the Civil War, but no one today was quite sure where. Legend had it that long before the war's end all that was left of Lottie was her voice, but its description varied. Lottie had walked into the North Carolina mountains from Tennessee with her two growing sons, unwilling to donate them to either army. Once up in the high country she had little need for her guns' protection, for the only residents besides native creatures were societal escapees like herself wishing to remain alone. Over the initial weeks of their seclusion, the motley denizens remained distant and aloof from one another, but after realizing life itself held more threats than they would to one another, now and then a man would travel off the mountain toward civilization and return with news.

Within the cave Lottie created a space for herself and the boys to hunker down and wait out the few months that those in charge—though she couldn't have said who—had predicted to achieve the South's success against the aggressive North. During daylight hours she felt the comfort of the den's pressing walls, but as the war dragged on her fears mixed at night with the cave's dark unknowns as well as the growing gloom and truth of the dawning future. In choosing the confines of the cave's visible and seemingly habitable boundaries, she confused protection with stupefaction and an easy malaise came over her. Though in no real danger of starving, Lottie began hoarding food, requiring her sons to hunt and kill far more game than the three could eat. Though the boys dressed the animals properly, their carcasses began to rot. Her sons, dreaming of creating Yankee corpses rather than dropping animal flesh, complained about the smell and refused to eat what their mother cooked over an open fire. Inexplicably, Lottie kept the extra provisions in a fetid pile in the cave, unable to relinquish the supply, as though it would become sustenance when her sons stopped complaining and manifested acceptance. How could they not see that the threats of the real world, rather than she, had imprisoned them?

But the cave, which clutched Lottie, presented a gaping portal to her boys. And one day during their mother's absence her two impatient sons, John Richard, seventeen, and Boyd Lee, sixteen, became embroiled in an argument, wanting to leave the monstrous smell and loneliness of the cave, their aim to become Tennessee war heroes. However, in their isolation they made the mistake of fighting each other rather than reasoning with their mother. As their argument escalated, John Richard managed to retrieve a gun from where Lottie had stored her idle cache. He only wounded his younger brother in the side, but a resentful Boyd Lee then grabbed the dropped gun from his brother's side and shot him dead. Stunned at his own actions, Boyd Lee's last remaining wits told him to run. He feared his mother's wrath.

Had he stayed to face Lottie that day, she could have tended him; instead, his wound festered and Lottie found his body five days later. It took her all day to drag her son's body back to the cave where she cradled him, first next to the dying fire as though to warm him, and then by the putrid pile of rotting meat, as though to nourish him. With the weight of her son's body on her torso her legs soon went numb. After some time her jaw dropped and the wind stole what was left of her reeking alluvial breath. Her mouth formed a slack O. Her head tipped back on inefficient neck muscles, her eyes fixed on the cave's blackened ceiling covered with grooves that wandered nowhere. Mother and son remained locked in a rigid embrace of tomblike safety while Lottie's incessant silent scream searched without result for her other combatant.

VALLEY OF FIRE

L ike a mother eyeing her children's display of bad behavior
from an unreachable distance away, Linda Ortiz stared from
the porch of her dingy trailer toward the casino. Between her
home and the gaming establishment lay a wide expanse of black
pavement, parking for the myriad patrons who whiled away
their non-wagering hours in the parking lot, especially on the
weekends when the casino stayed open all night, encouraging
those who gambled and drank to gamble and drink even more.
Only five years ago her trailer had sat here at the head of the
road leading to the Valley of Fire and she'd felt like a caretaker,
even though Nevada's Division of State Parks hardly knew of
her existence. How was it that here in Overton, an hour north-
east of Las Vegas, with 36,000 acres of state park to her left and
shimmering desert expanse to her right, she could now feel so
cramped beside the small structure? If only Billy had lived she
wouldn't be in this fix. He had died too young, alcohol rotting
his gut. But she couldn't dwell on that now. She had to make
the best of the casino's moving in five years ago, *encroaching*

she wanted to say though she had to admit the developers had not given her even the smallest reason to complain at the time with their vigilance concerning debris and deed lines during construction. Ten years ago, when Overton had first floated the idea of the casino's placement, Linda and Billy had felt sure the town council would choose a more central location appealing to the Las Vegas crowd than the remote entrance to the distant Valley of Fire, but instead a monster had been born aside the Ortiz yard.

At one time Linda's trailer glowed a singular bright white in the brilliant desert sun. She felt it had been a lighthouse of sorts, shining like a promise to tourists who would rumble down the long two-lane road running before her home on their way toward the entrance to the Valley of Fire. However, the casino's twenty-four-hour red and yellow blinking illumination had gradually dimmed her home's presentation and she damned the developers after they left. Equal culprits in the decline of her home were the constantly blowing sands and the punishing sun, but these were elements of destruction she accepted given her love of the desert.

·   ·   ·

"I want to see Christmas Tree Pass."

"Don't expect Christmas trees, you dope." Micky stuck his tongue out at his younger sister Misty.

"Then why is it called Christmas Tree Pass, Mr. Desert Expert?"

Micky, as usual, had anticipated his gullible sister's question and already fabricated an answer: "Long ago the Indians used to move pine trees through this area—"

"The desert?" Even Misty at nine years old was incredulous.

"—for Christmas, stupid. They aren't *grown* here, o-b-v-i-o-u-s-l-y. They come from other places, like Mexico, which is really close. How else would the Indians get trees into their tee-pees for the holidays?"

The clearly observable evidence that Christmas trees were *not* grown in the desert gave Misty pause and she calculated her next comment so as not to confirm her idiocy when compared to her older brother.

She tried a different tactic. "Well, I just don't know where they would have bought their ornaments."

Marcy and Len Menham listened to their children sitting in the back seat of the '99 Jeep without remark, Len's jaw rigidly set as he drove. He and Marcy were used to this incessant commentary and the heat was not improving matters. Inside the picnic basket sitting on Marcy's lap the food was deteriorating; in fact, without working air conditioning in the car they were all deteriorating. The basket was far too large and should have been stored in the back of the vehicle, in the trunk space beyond the children's narrow shoulders, but she knew their wandering hands would have meandered toward the basket's two latches, finding ways to pilfer with impunity whatever they could. They were like that—and always in competition at less than a year apart. She and Len had had the kids too close, with their names too closely related as well, as though forcing a sibling relationship. If she could do it over again she would have planned them years apart. Then they would have cared for one another.

"Where's the entrance?" asked Misty. "The sign said we were at the entrance to the Fire Valley."

"*Valley* of Fire," corrected her brother.

"Entrances out west can seem different than in the east. They have a lot more space here," explained their mother.

"Look at that house." Micky pointed to the right, his arm dangling languidly out the car's window until it dropped with a thud against the door's exterior. "It needs paint. Is that different out here too, Mom, how they use paint? Who would live here anyway?" The boy had no idea that until the casino's opening Linda Ortiz had felt like a model citizen of desert life, a year-round spring cactus bloom, with her neat yard surrounding her alabaster beacon of a home amidst the sand and tumble-weed. In years past her property alone had been the tourists' focus as they entered the park, a sacred place to her and those gone before her. Aware of its entire map of edges, curves, and blemishes, or so she felt, she claimed a kind of spiritual owner-ship of the park and lived in peace with the innocent creatures, variant winds, and prickly vegetation. Every mote of the park was protected, but on her explorations she still strove to touch the entirety of the deep red sandstone within her reach. To walk in the footsteps of the ancient people who had lived there was not difficult and she would frequently stop by a rock's picto-graphs, close her eyes, and breathe deeply, especially after Billy's death. But if communication is difficult amongst the living, it is even more so with the dead. She felt weak as a communal spirit, only able to futilely imagine responding to the silent ancient rock art with petroglyphs of her own.

"And a casino!" shrieked Misty. "They have games there." She looked back and forth excitedly between the casino's lights and what she could see of her father's face in the front seat.

Suddenly Len leaned over and fairly shouted into his wife's ear, "Look at the eagle!"

Marcy pushed her husband back toward the steering wheel. "You're making me deaf. Now I won't be able to hear the des-ert." She rubbed her aching ear. "You've made my ear sting, Len. And you nearly knocked over the picnic basket. You've got to drive *properly*."

"What's to hear in the desert, Mom?" asked Misty, leaning forward, eager to spy the eagle in the sky.

Micky seized the opening: "Coyotes and bears and ruskrats—"

"That would be *muskrats*, Mick," Len corrected, "but I don't think muskrats are here."

Hardly caring, Micky continued, "—and giant hawks and ghosts. Lots of ghosts of old Indians that sneak up on cars, especially tourist cars, and scare little girls."

From the back Len heard, "Can't we drive faster?" He hadn't discerned which of his children had asked him to pick up the pace, but it didn't matter since either could have lodged the complaint.

By now Micky had unbuckled his seatbelt and crept closer to his sister, violating the invisible dividing line drawn between them, half the bench seat for one, half the bench seat for the other, neither crossing even while napping. Behind her mother's scat Misty searched the sky for the soaring eagle through the open window. Repositioning herself to relieve stress on her neck she abruptly realized her brother's proximity and screamed a set of high notes accessed as ammunition only by those under ten on a playground.

"Now I'm deaf in *both* ears," claimed their mother, clutching each with a hand as the picnic basket slammed into the passenger door. Soon something began to leak onto her bare thigh.

"Here we are in a place of culture," charged Len, "and all of you have to become unhinged. Imagine if we were being filmed. No one would nominate us for Family of the Month this month."

"Not any month," mumbled his wife, her head and upper torso creating a right angle toward the open window as she strained to search under the basket for the cause of the liquid dampening her skin, but given the basket's width and weight, she could hardly expect to view its bottom.

Len licked his left index finger and located a place on the windshield to deposit his spit and rub.

"What the hell are you doing?" asked Marcy. "I asked you not to clean spots that way. It's disgusting."

"Is that a show?" shouted Misty.

"Is what a show?" asked Len.

"Family of the Month. Could we apply and be on TV? Really, *really* be on TV?"

"I want to be on TV," cried out Micky. "I want my friends to see me."

"Can I wear makeup, *pleeease*, Mom?" implored Misty. "All my friends wear makeup and you won't let me. Just this one time, kay?"

"Your friends do not wear makeup, Misty. Your friends are nine-year-old little girls. Although sometimes I think their mothers are merely ten-year-old girls—"

"Marcy!" cut in Len, "not in front of the kids."

Micky wanted to return to the issue at hand. "So when can we be on the show?"

"What show?" asked Len again, forgetting already.

"*There is no show*. Your dad made it up." Marcy glowered at Len.

"But you got my hopes up."

"Mine toooo," added Misty, echoing her brother's tone as the dissonance in their voices met and then sharpened.

In annoyance Marcy violently turned her torso toward the back seat, again upsetting the picnic basket on her lap. She was about to rebuke her children but instead she had thrown the basket into Len's shoulder and this time its contents created a loud clank as they collided.

"*OW!* Now look what you've done," protested Len as he slowed the Jeep with a mad slam of his foot on the brake. "You've ruined my lunch."

"*Your* lunch. Like there aren't others in this car? Plus, lunch can be replaced," explained Marcy, fiddling for one of the basket's latches. "You might be more concerned about grandma's dishes instead."

"What the hell did you bring the old lady's good dishes for? No wonder that thing was so heavy when I dragged it out to the car this morning."

Marcy forgot the latch. "I thought they'd add to our nature outing," she huffed. "Grandma's dishes are beautiful."

"But not for picnics."

Behind their parents Mick and Mindy made sport of their parents' spat, turning away from one another periodically to assemble grotesque faces with which to then leer at one another.

Len gave up trying to reason with his wife and asked, "And have any of you taken a look at the god damn eagle?"

"*Len*, no swearing."

"But you did, Mom," clarified Misty. She relaxed the current foolish facial expression she had aimed at her brother.

"Your swearing, it's like with that woman in the grocery parking lot the other day," Marcy suddenly fired at Len.

Len seemed hurt. "But you said she didn't stop at the intersection and almost ran you down."

"Did you go after her, Mom?" asked Micky with renewed breathless anticipation, forgetting the pursuit of the eagle.

"No, of course not, though I did remark on her unsafe driving skills as she passed me. As it happens, her passenger window was open. I don't think she realized she had scared me. I never would have walked forward across the lanes had I known she wouldn't make a proper stop. That's why you children should always—"

"Did she come after you?" Micky hoped for a less methodical response from his mother this time around.

"As a matter of fact she did. She found me in the grocery aisles and told me I had ruined her day by pointing out her mistake. Imagine that, I had ruined *her* day."

"But she made the mistake and could have hurt you," summed up Misty.

"And that would not have made *my* day, would it?"

"She was an idiot," added Len callously, as if the children needed clarification.

"But you didn't need to call her 'fucking crazy' right there in the aisle," whispered Marcy, though the children were all ears. "You only agitated her."

"I was there to protect you."

"By swearing? You made it your issue when it was mine." Marcy stared forward into the desert. "One shouldn't swear until sworn at."

"Then no one would swear."

"Exactly."

"Except you did too, Mom, a minute ago," pestered Misty.

"And so did Dad," confirmed Micky.

Len looked at his wife and shrugged. "Dead to rights. Case closed."

Misty resumed straining her neck even more out the car's window. "I can't see the eagle in the air."

Micky grabbed the headrest atop his father's seat, yanking Len back. His father's foot fell back off the gas pedal and then heavily hit it again, jerking the car forward.

"I *told* you to drive properly," reminded Marcy. "This is why I don't like you driving my car. I'm trying to save it."

Len ignored his wife while rubbing his neck. "It's not in the air, sweetie," he answered his daughter concerning the eagle's location. "It's still perched on that rock ahead. Notice how quiet it can be. Let's see if we can all be—"

Micky grabbed ahold of the front seats like an athlete about to mount a gymnast's horse and shot his head and shoulders between his parents, but Len roughly shoved his son with the back of his elbow. Micky expelled a throaty "Uuchhh" as he hit the back seat again, to which Misty responded with a satisfied smirk.

"Well, you could have been more clear," snapped Marcy, "putting us all through calisthenics to find the thing. We'll all need rehab soon enough between your driving and craning our necks to find specimens of nature."

Once the eagle had been located in such a low and unexciting spot, on a mere rock, it was swiftly deemed too immobile by the children to be of interest. In fact, the entire park was failing to capture the imagination of any particular member of the Menham family. It offered only the brown sameness seen when driving most of Nevada's miles, though every once in a while a red rock popped up. *Valley of Fire?*, mused Marcy. Perhaps from above the area looks ringed with red formations.

"My foot is splitting, Mom," declared Misty.

Micky gazed with interest toward his sister's bare foot, hoping for a bizarre scene more worthy of his time than some stock-still eagle, but he was disappointed to find Misty's skin and toes intact.

"What are you talking about?" asked her mother.

"Remember that Pyrex dish that fell on my foot?" She made the fact sound like a complaint.

"Turned it that purple-blue," recalled Micky with relish. "A real mash smash. Man, that subterranean blood mushed out all over your foot underneath your skin."

"What's the problem now?" Marcy asked with a certain resignation in her voice.

"The two big toes are growing away from the little three."

"Maybe we'll see a doctor once we're back home," Marcy consoled, knowing they would not. The child had been x-rayed and no broken bone had been found. She was fine.

"What if I can't wear proper shoes when we go on *Family of the Month*. What if I can't walk by then?"

"Good gracious." Marcy was exasperated. "I told you your father made that show up."

"I didn't make up a show. I just employed the term abstractly."

"Well, the children don't know what's abstract and what's concrete."

"I know we walk on concrete," offered Misty helpfully.

"Not the same. Now let's be more quiet," suggested Marcy. "We're coming near the park's entrance. We came here to make memories."

"What kind?" asked the children simultaneously.

"Good question," mouthed Len as he approached a small covered kiosk and stopped to pay the park's entrance fee, then gently moving the vehicle forward again.

"Can't you try to get the air conditioning to work, Len? It's just stifling out here."

"I told you we shouldn't come to the desert without A/C."

"Well, just think of all those who did a century ago and lived to tell about it," snapped Marcy as though this were a scientific explanation.

Those people were used to dealing without air conditioning, considered Len, quite rationally he thought, though he kept his mouth shut. *The damn mechanisms hadn't been invented yet.*

Behind Len his son was bored. Nothing encountered so far was worthy of conveying to friends once home. The Valley of Fire offered little of note, just a winding road through periodic dirt mounds. Given the park's name, he had hoped for multiple wild conflagrations, but he hadn't seen anything approaching even a campfire in size. He would even have endured standing on one of the stupid mounds that were everywhere and viewing a display of faraway heat and flame at this point.

"Len, I need you to stop the car."

"Now?"

"Now."

"But what for?"

"I'm having one of those pain spasms in my back."

"Now?"

"Yes, now."

"And what will stopping the car do?"

"You'll need to draw an X on the spot."

"Now?"

"*Yes*, now."

"But I'm driving the car."

"Which means you can stop the car. A car can stop."

"But we're in the middle of the road."

"No one's here. Now stop the car." Marcy reached forward to the Jeep's cup holder where she always kept a black pen. She lifted up her shirt in the back and awkwardly pointed to indicate her pain, but all Len saw was his wife's twisted palm with its thumb thrust upward. "Here. Draw here," Marcy insisted.

Len did as he was told, but Marcy claimed his pen had been misplaced. "Try again. See, right here. I can feel you're not in the right place."

The individual reeds of the basket's weave poked uncomfortably into his wife's chest and she would not sit still. Still, Len again followed instructions and marveled at the mess of ink marks he had created on his wife's skin, at her request no less.

"What happens when you shower later?"

"You'll just have to do it again. And then again the next day, until I get an appointment with Dr. Blaney. I can talk to him about the Alzheimer's thing too."

"What Alzheimer's thing?"

"Well, I find myself forgetting things."

"Ha, if I needed a doctor for that I'd already be put away in some unit," laughed Len. "Everyone forgets stuff."

"It's gotten more acute, the idea I mean, not the forgetting, since that woman erroneously called our house last week thinking she had left a message about her hospitalized mother's health condition. She was updating someone in an important way about her own dear mother and she didn't even know that

I, a perfect stranger, was receiving the message instead. I feel like I should have called her or brought her food or something."

"But you don't even know her."

"Plus, I erased all those messages," piped in Misty from behind her mother.

"Whatever for? What if I had needed to keep those messages, young lady?"

"Isn't a message done with once you've listened to it?"

Len had to smile at his daughter's logic, but Misty looked down at her hands to avoid the half of her mother's glaring face turned toward her. "And I think I did it accidentally too." Her voice trailed off.

Micky just stared at his sister. She was in enough hot water that he didn't even need to participate in this one and risk implicating himself.

"Look *there*," cried Misty. "It's a coyote."

"Why I think it is," confirmed Len. "But—" The animal had a strange look. It lay at the side of the road and gazed without recognition at the steel danger nearing that was the Menhams' vehicle.

"I don't think that animal looks healthy," whispered Marcy as a warning.

"Gotcha." He glanced at his children using the rear view mirror. "We'll just slow down and take a look from the car, but I need you to roll up your windows."

Misty dutifully complied with her father's request, but Micky found the notion ridiculous. "It's six hundred degrees out, Dad. You can't be *serious*."

This time Len glared into the rear view mirror and Micky changed his attitude, but by then Len had driven past the coyote and wavered to the left side of the road into the oncoming lane.

"What is that smell?" asked Len. "It's like vinegar. What broke in that basket, Marcy?"

"I think it's okay to back up," reassured his wife. "No one's around."

Len put the car in reverse and tried to straighten out the Jeep as he looked to his left for the coyote. It was probably dying and he didn't want to run the thing over. But in all his care the car made a grinding sound.

"Clearly that was bad. The car never did that for me," accused Marcy.

"How often do you back up and turn sharply?"

"At the same time? What a weird question. How do I know?"

"Well, the car made the same sound in the motel's parking lot before I came around to pick you all up at the lobby entrance. I think it's the differential."

"Are you saying I wrecked the car?"

"I'm not saying that at all. I'm saying our differential may be going. Although I do feel you might have paid more attention to the Freon level. We might not be sweltering at this moment."

"Obviously the Freon leaked out and blew away."

"That's not how Freon works, Marcy."

"Then how does it work?"

"Well, first—"

"The coyote!" shouted Mindy. "It's moving."

"And we," Len abruptly stopped the car, "are not going to find out where to. This encounter with nature is over." Len moved forward rather quickly into the proper lane, slowly realizing no car had tried to pass them either way since they had paid their entrance fee. As all four reopened their windows, Len felt the park suddenly turn lonely and its atmosphere eerily ominous. If park officials didn't know a coyote was sick and dying right here on the road, what else didn't they know?

"Let's drive a few more miles and then stop for lunch," suggested Marcy, who still looked forward to finding out what was keeping her leg so damp. "We should also stop at some of these mounds. After all, this is supposed to be an educational experience. We've come a long way from a different climate and I made us nice sandwiches at the motel this morning."

"It's summer vacation," noted Micky, "so we don't have to learn again until school starts."

"Glad to know we're raising such an intellectual." Len threw the words from the side of his mouth over to his wife, but Marcy was scanning the park's brochure.

"Stop here, Len. These are supposed to be the Beehives, children, ancient sand formations." She began to read verbatim from the pamphlet's pages, words which Micky and Misty immediately tuned out.

"I think I want to be a park attendant when I grow up," Micky announced. Len sighed at his son's latest stated aspiration. The previous week Micky had declared his desire to be a starship trooper. "There's nothing much to do here, but I'd get to deal with the coyotes."

"Can I be your partner?" asked Misty, evincing strange admiration for the brother she spent more time sparring with in life than loving.

"No."

Len pulled into the small paved arc of parking space placed before the Beehives area for visitors. "Here we go. Everyone out. Marcy, I'll come over there and take that basket from your lap."

"Thank god. My butt is swimming in sweat and the top of my thighs are covered with goo."

The children had exited like lightening, hoping for any sort of breeze compared with the stagnant air in the car. Len made his way to the passenger side of the Jeep and lifted the basket from his wife's lap, bending his knees deeply to help his back absorb the weight. He eyed the expanse of burnt desert dust beyond the pavement in search of a picnic table.

"I don't see any wind," complained Misty, "and I crave wind."

Micky's eyebrows seemed to meet along his forehead as he pondered his sister's remark. "No one sees the wind and no one craves wind either."

"Well, I crave some lunch," said their mother now standing outside the car and examining her thighs. "Follow your father." Between the oppressive heat and the leak she felt the need for head-to-toe sanitation. Whatever had seeped through the basket was oily as well as sticky.

"Let's do the mounds first," Len offered, "while your mother sets out lunch." For the first time that day Marcy gave her husband a look of gratitude. Misty quickly took her father's hand but then yanked it away at its stickiness. Micky strutted beside them independently a good four feet away. Len wiped his hands repeatedly on his white shorts, leaving dark smears.

"They're kind of stupid," Micky summed up once they'd reached the formations.

"Well, they've been eroded by wind and water over thousands of years," explained their father feebly. "You'd look a little less than fresh after that kind of beating too."

Len stood at one mound's edge and leaned forward while Misty trekked boldly to the top.

"Don't stand on the mound," tormented Micky. "Ghosts live there and will get squeezed out."

"So here's a mound," confirmed Len, as though his children might miss it. "And there's another," not even really pointing to any specific second rise in the ground. The three fell silent. "Well, I think your mother must have lunch ready by now."

Misty stamped her feet and then kicked. "Good, cuz these tumbleweed things are biting my legs."

Back at the picnic table Marcy had opened the basket's lid slowly, afraid of what sort of jumble she would discover. Relieved to find her grandmother's dishes securely strapped in on the left, just as they had been in the motel, the top plate's clean and shiny appearance revealed nothing in the way of the leaking culprit within. She poked around the carefully packed items to the right, lifting sticky plastic containers and picking through levels of various foods items wrapped like gifts in stained wax paper. Several times she rubbed her fingers together as though the stickiness would go away. And then she found it: the plastic cover to a jar containing honey balsamic vinaigrette had cracked in two, allowing the contents to carelessly spill upward and outward within the basket without discrimination. In addition, the fruits of the desert were beginning to plague her physically, two small tumbleweed spheres suddenly blowing up against her ankles, their barbs scraping her skin, goading her agitation. Yet she would have to make the best of the situation considering she saw Len and the children walking toward her. She sighed at the untamed appearance of Micky and Misty and the state of her husband's shorts.

"How were the mounds?" she called out, receiving no answer.

"What's for lunch?" asked Micky as he hopped onto the bench seat opposite his mother.

"Well, we're going to have to be a little careful, guys. We've had a slight spill."

"You mean *you* had a spill, Mom," corrected Micky. "You're the one in charge of the food all the time."

Marcy handed out individually wrapped sandwiches as Len and Misty seated themselves, Misty beside her brother and Len across from his daughter.

"What's wrong with this?" moaned Misty as soon as she encountered the damp wax paper swaddling. "I can't even touch the paper. I think I'm infected."

"Mine's all stuck together," chimed in Micky. "Look, I can't even unwrap it."

By now Misty had exposed her sandwich and the balsamic-stained bread. "I can't eat *this*," she declared. "It's got dirt on it." She held the fully removed wax paper sheet aloft as though it were toxic.

"That's not dirt," assured her mother, "just a little vinegar."

"Vinegar is used on cat piss," Misty announced. She crumpled the wax paper and shoved it into the pocket of her shorts. She would make her mother find it later in the wash.

"*Misty!*" cried her mother.

Rather than rebuke his daughter, Len valiantly bit into his sandwich in an effort to demonstrate its benign qualities, but he quivered as he did since he had always shunned vinegars of any kind. The tartness of the condiment instantly made his eyes water, an odd occurrence, he noted, in the desert heat.

Micky pushed his own sandwich forward toward his mother with a single finger. "I'll just have the potato salad you bought."

"*May* I have the potato salad?" suggested his father tersely, which caused Micky to hand the container to his father once his mother had retrieved it from the basket.

"That's not what I meant," growled Len.

"Then don't ask for it, Dad." But the potato salad was a disappointment too, bleeding trails of balsamic appearing on the surface as well where the plastic cover, shoved aside during one of the basket's upsets, had accepted a quantity of the vinaigrette. "What *can* we eat?" whined Micky.

The four sat strangely paralyzed. "The dishes …" Marcy said vaguely, recalling her need to bring her grandmother's heavy plates.

"This is as bad as Mrs. Crashtree's food," pronounced Misty as she spun herself around on the bench to face away from her parents.

"Who is Crashtree?" asked Len.

"Our new neighbor, two doors down," informed his wife. "And when did you eat their food? I don't remember giving permission."

"It was just cookies, and they were awful."

"You mean cookies that could ruin your dinner?"

"Let it go, Marcy," said Len. "It must have been days ago. And how come I don't know about this Crashtree person. Whose name is Crashtree anyway?"

"I believe it's Crabtree, Misty," suggested Marcy, "isn't it?"

"Crashtree," confirmed Micky.

"And she's looking for a man," revealed Misty, as her mother gasped and put a hand to her mouth. "She said she's *rea DEE*. That's how she put it, *rea DEE* for a man."

"Who says such things to children, Len?"

"She won't be getting that man," said Micky, "cause her nostrils are too large. I could look right up into them when she talked."

"Plus, Mom would call them barbarians," inserted Misty, "because they salt their food before eating it. At least her kids do."

"She has children? And I thought you only ate cookies—"

"Two."

"Two cookies or two children?" asked Len.

"Two kids, but Gardinia said she had a third baby once but it was born sleeping."

Well, at least that information came out with some delicacy, thought Len.

"Misty! You must call her Mrs. Crashtree, not Gardinia."

"But she told us—"

"And I'm telling you now otherwise."

"I don't know as she'll get married because of her purple hair either," added Micky suddenly recalling vital information.

"Plus, she'll die of Alzheimer's. Her mother did, so she will too. She told us."

"*What?*" Now Len had had enough. "People don't die of Alzheimer's. See what your own irrational fears have done to the children's thinking, Marcy? I believe it's time to pack up and enjoy the rest of the park," he announced with mock cheerfulness.

"But we're *HUN*-gry," wailed the children almost simultaneously.

"Okay, we can pick up some ice cream later in the park."

"Len, this is a state park, not an amusement park."

"Well, it may be a state park, but I'm stating they have nothing much here at all. The least they could do is offer some treats."

"That's great. Just go ahead and buy into this attitude of the children's." Marcy began slamming containers back into the basket without any of the geometric precision she had used hours earlier in the motel. "We came here for an educational and cultural experience and I don't see us having one."

"Nor do I," confirmed Len as he rose from the table and feigned the appearance of being helpful by lining up the soggy food items that had sat before the children, every once in a while wiping his fingers off on his thighs.

"Look what you're doing to your shorts, Len. They've become streaked."

"How else do you think I can get rid of this stuff?" Len wet his index finger in his mouth and tried altering one of the smudges, rubbing hard.

"Like that is going to help. It will never come out."

"There's more shorts at the store," offered Misty. "You can just buy some."

"Can we walk in the slipstream?" asked Micky, blithely accepting the meal's sudden end.

Marcy stared at her son. "What slipstream?"

"It's the air behind a moving vehicle." He puffed out his chest as his sister looked on with undue adoration. "We learned about it in school. It should pull us along."

"A slipstream is created by a jet propeller, son, not a slow moving Jeep." Len felt all he did these days was correct his various family members.

"Just drive faster then."

"Even if I did, you couldn't walk that fast, silly. Can you see how your idea is ridiculous?"

"*Len!*, I don't think the children's ideas should ever be deemed ridiculous in their presence. What will it do to their self-esteem?"

"Perhaps they'll learn that some ideas are worthy and some," he paused and looked directly in Marcy's eyes, "*are not.* Now let's get going."

"Okay then, but we are driving right out of here," directed Marcy, "not completing this park but going back out through the very entrance where we arrived. I can't finish this."

For a moment a pall was cast. As the four made their way back to the car, each dawdled, ironically feeling the weight of the uneaten food, whether by its lingering presence in the basket or the knowledge of its never having been consumed. Yet, with the prospect of the car's stifling atmosphere and the mindless miles ahead of them, getting the children back into their seats suddenly became like dragging two goats through a tin can patch. Micky and Misty began to chase the ubiquitous tumbleweed and laughed as though finally enjoying their outing.

"Let's take this one home," commanded Misty, holding up a substantial but weightless globe of tangled tumbleweed vines.

"Fine," acquiesced their mother. She would have given permission to return with an elephant. She wanted the day to be over, not knowing yet she would listen for the next hour to her children fight over where the tumbleweed should sit between them to avoid its thorns.

Marcy only knew it would *not* sit up front.

.   .   .

The day had been quiet and Linda Ortiz happened to catch the Menhams' exit just as she had noticed their Jeep's passing earlier that morning. She had been about to wave, as she liked to do, when she saw the little girl in the back seat lean an arm out the window and carelessly drop a darkly stained piece of paper onto the road. Linda's face clouded with despair. Just then one of thousands of prickly tumbleweeds, scattering its propagules without regard to boundaries, blew across Linda's yard. Their sting was brief but the grip unrelenting.

TAKING DOWN THE MOON

The moon was too bright so Cleo called out to his mother from his bedroom. She arrived, anxious at his tone and wiping her damp hands on the checkered apron tied neatly around her waist.

"The moon ... it's too bright," Cleo complained. "I can't sleep. Could you take down the moon?"

His mother, marking the moon's abundant light filling the spaces of the room with rude abandon, did not even bother to lift the window from the sill. Instead, she smiled and reached right through the glass of her son's bedroom window. The glass gave against the pressure as though her hands pushed through sand. Near her hip the top drawer of the boy's nightstand opened obediently, its contents—jacks and small balls and tiny green soldiers—noisily receding. The mother reached a bit further into the night air and then into the inky expanse. She had stretched so far all that seemed left of her were her legs and feet, still firmly placed on the wood floor. The soldiers of the drawer rattled in fear; the window's glass bore invisible scars. When

Cleo again saw his mother's face it shone from the strain, but in her hands she balanced the great sphere, the night's stars dangling as if tethered by strings, wearied by the journey. Merely by looking at her the boy knew the moon's weight and loved his mother more than ever, realizing her sway and control. The orb must have been scorching her hands, but she did not flinch.

The mother deftly tucked the moon with its brilliance into the boy's open drawer and resolutely closed it, even though the moon's last rays fought to illuminate the room. She let the stars, with their insistent twinkling, fall securely to the middle drawer. Tomorrow morning she would retrieve the sun from the bottom drawer and toss the dazzling blaze into an importuning sky to create the dawn.

ESSA

1988

Ever since Essa had come back from the dead she could sing. High notes. Low notes. She was a regular Ella Fitzgerald. Some folks even thought themselves witty by calling Essa Ella.

"Knock that off, Sylamine," Nadine would say tersely to her neighbor.

"Well, it's not like she came with a name tag."

But Essa wasn't black. And she wasn't quite white either. Later, those less enamored with her on Gate Mountain in the small community of Ethan called her "not right" because she didn't fit. But Nadine knew their feelings stemmed from simple jealously. Essa had roots elsewhere, though no one could say where. And as much as Nadine wanted to keep her, Essa's appearance in Ethan proved she was capable of transplanting herself again, a fact Nadine found both fearful and gratifying.

Essa would get out. The rest were stuck.

Essa had olive skin and jet black hair which swarmed around her head in an unruly mess even when freshly combed.

Some keenly observant folks of Ethan found Essa's hands and feet remarkably small and decided, soon after her appearance, that she came from a world of little physical work and responsibility. Those romantic enough speculated that she must have been the fairy daughter of a demon prince and a defiled damsel—or at least an heiress cut off by a scheming second wife hoping to move Essa out of the way.

But no one knew who she was. And she couldn't stay without a name.

In Ethan when a woman found herself pregnant, it was common to shout names out the back door. It was a way of settling on the right one. If you tire of one, don't let it return, people would say. Just keep the ones you don't mind inviting back in. But Essa had just appeared. People called her a sudden child. There had been no chewing over her arrival and no calling of names. No woman of Ethan had been pregnant nine long months, enduring prickly anticipation and lamenting thwarted time. In fact, no one had thought of her at all—and then, unexpectedly, she was *here*. As such, at first no one knew what to do with her. Then no one knew what to name her. However, they knew she must be kept.

And Essa wasn't dead when found either; nor did she return from the dead as some who were inclined toward drama in the community liked to say. She had been found asleep along the rural mountain road to Ethan. Nadine had spotted her while cutting errant tiger lilies from the ditch a ways from her home. Dressed in muted pink, from a distance the little girl had looked more like a dropped rag. Nadine's eyes had easily passed over the formless heap in her quest for the blaze orange lilies. Though they would bloom only a day, she had planned a lunch that afternoon—the term luncheon seeming too proper—and wanted spots of color to splatter her drab living room. *Splatter* had been the word that caught her eye. At work she had recently flipped through a homes magazine, stopping to read a blurb on brightening up rooms. *Be daring*, it had proposed. *Lighten, brighten, whiten* suggested the writer of the article. Common daisies, left on the longest of stems, crowded the floor's corners of the photographed room, spread out gloriously on the following two pages. The pictures had excited Nadine. Though Nadine's living room looked nothing like the opulent room shown on the glossy pages, its textures, hues, and lighting suddenly became more real to her than her own dim corners. The magazine daisies filled spaces on the mantel over the fireplace, a spot on each end table—daringly off center no less—and even upside down from the ceiling fan. Who has that many vases Nadine wondered. And how did one get a bag of water to stay up there near the ceiling fan?

Lighten, brighten, whiten ... Then enlighten! fairly shouted the editors from the article's conclusion. Nadine didn't know how flowers enlightened, or whether she was supposed to do the enlightening herself, but here in the ditch she did feel particularly clever, having reversed the writer's color scheme suggestion to suit her own needs. The author had assumed the presence of vivid color in her readers' living rooms, requiring the compliment of overly white daisies, but Nadine would instead introduce some flash into her faded living room environment with the lilies' flame. She gazed at the bouquet in her arms, now bending away from her under its own weight.

She had been musing over her inventiveness while in the ditch when she saw the dusty pink, C-shaped rag stir. Had the wind moved its folds? What were the wild dark strings at one end? And then she saw the child's face. In an instant Nadine rushed forward and scooped up the inert lump, leaving her thrillingly orange bouquet behind.

.   .   .

A small patch of the more hopeful of Ethan's residents derived Essa's name from the one consistent verbal emission she made after returning from the dead, many not letting go of this death connection for a good long time, a combination of *s* sounds which, of course, was just the result of the babble of a hungry but nonverbal and clearly exhausted child, but which the more optimistic in town claimed was her attempt to form the word princess or, if not that exciting, at least heiress.

Hogwash, thought Nadine.

"She's probably just clearing dust from her nose," she affirmed a half hour later from her own front yard, the mysterious child in her arms and the scheduled lunch having been summarily canceled. She had summoned Sylamine and Vincent only, but Sylamine had slyly made several phone calls herself before running next door to Nadine's. A small group of people had therefore assembled in Nadine's gravel driveway. With the discharge of an enormous sneeze, the child finally opened her eyelids to reveal bright pools of blue. Such clarity contrasted with her dusty face and wild black hair, giving her the look of a tiny chimney sweep.

No one else in Ethan needed the little girl. Vincent O'Dell had a grown son elsewhere and, he said firmly, only liked small children on a "case-by-case basis." Rose Sharon Darliss already had five young children, which constantly orbited around her, and who knew what else she and her husband would produce. Plus, everyone could already see her eldest, even at nine years old, wouldn't amount to anything, so what sort of future was there for the rest, let alone any innocent additions? Sylamine Teaberry said she dealt daily with her husband and affirmed, with arms folded firmly across her chest, that *that* was enough. And frail old Doc Spray, ironically with the largest home in the area, did not count. Of course there were others, but their silence clearly indicated their approval of Nadine's immediate parenthood, no one at that time giving a thought to a frantic family outside of Ethan or county authorities already considering the missing child part of their case load.

According to Nadine herself she had sworn off men some years ago ever since her sister's husband, fifty-two at the time, had surprised his young bride in the shower by sticking his hand unexpectedly through the shower curtain in an attempt to squeeze her firm but wet breast. Surprised, Nadine's sister had slipped, hit her head, and died instantly. Nadine didn't need any trouble of this kind from men. She did however need someone—she was thirty after all—and that someone became Essa.

Nadine named her daughter Essa not because of the conclusions of Ethan's citizens concerning sibilance but because Essa instantly rooted inside Nadine and became her essence. She hadn't set out to claim Essa's marrow; instead, quite quickly Essa settled into the corners and niches of Nadine's core and grew strong and permanent within her. Any difficulties ensued later when Essa, striving to grow up, began to reclaim herself. Then Nadine, who had acquired Essa's essence rather than discovering her own, could only painfully lose what was not hers bit by bit over time as her daughter constructed herself. By the time Essa was to leave, Nadine was incapable of recognizing that she had cultivated no spirit of her own. But these troubles would all come later. First Essa had to grow up.

As a child Essa was a wild exaggerator. In response to some chore put in front of her, she might complain, "But that will take a hundred million hours." Given her lunch she would look with disbelief at a steaming bowl of soup, announce that a thousand degrees was just too hot for her delicate throat and ask sarcastically for an accompanying bucket of ice. She exasperated Nadine.

In the church choir Essa would be asked to sing the highest of parts, and being paired with Essa always meant being second. Yet in a petulant manner, or so thought her patient fellow choir members, Essa would claim that *no one* could sing sixty-eight octaves above C. But her fellow choir members couldn't dislike her. If Essa's partner was scolded by the choir director as singing off key, Essa would urge reassuringly, "You're not singing flat, you're just on the sad side of the note."

Essa could also be outrageously imaginative. One morning Nadine came into the living room to find its brown shag rug covered in a profusion of half-inch colored shavings. The uncountable motley peelings seemed to balance atop the frayed tips of old rug's threads and ran a careful but strange path around the furniture of the room. As she walked onto the carpet, Nadine felt the pieces glue themselves to the bottoms of her feet like clippings from a newly mown lawn.

"*Ess-ssa!*"

After bounding into the room, Essa explained without a morsel of remorse that she had been "feeding the fish," having seen each strand of shag carpct from the eye of a six-year-old angler.

"I took the crayon sharpener," she said, and here she opened her hand and showed her mother the now extracted small rectangular sharpener included inside each box of sixty-four or more Crayola Crayons, "and fed the fish—like this," and she demonstrated by walking around the room and twirling her hand in an invisible shaver, mocking her own earlier movements.

Discovered in the road weeds at approximately a year old, or so determined Doc Spray, who died just days later and had never thought to call the Department of Social Services or make a record of his initial appointments with Nadine's foundling, Essa took her sweet time learning to speak, preferring instead to emit her *s* sound as though it was the only soothing element she had brought from where ever she had come from and she couldn't let go. Once she did speak she did so sparingly but could be utterly insistent when she did. One cold afternoon at around two years old she asked repeatedly for "peach of pocket." Nadine tried for hours to convince her daughter that she had no peaches, that peaches weren't even in season, and that peaches did not belong in pockets anyway. It was early evening before she realized Essa, still imploring her mother firmly for "peach of pocket," wanted a p-i-e-c-e o-f c-h-o-c-o-l-a-t-e. She ate the piece and fell silent again.

Until she sang. When small she had created songs about bugs and snakes and turtles and as an adolescent she had hummed eerie tunes no one had ever heard. But she sang in the church choir, crystal clear notes that seemed to soar to Heaven and made listeners close their eyes, bow as if in prayer, and be ever more thankful for God's intangibles, like the gift of sound; yet Essa did not bow her own head during prayer, a fact gone mercifully unnoticed by the meditating devout.

Essa may have been unlike her fellow Ethan residents, but she was no fool. Upon returning from elementary school every afternoon she would find an apple or simple crackers and uncharacteristically (for most children) sit down at the kitchen table and open her books. This devotion to learning carried itself into high school. As the frequency of her questions increased with her daughter's rapid intellectual maturity, Nadine would hide her ignorance with the same encouraging response: "You can grow up and figure out how that's done." But one day Essa declared *all* of high school "figured out," leaving Nadine at a loss. Later during one of their many long-running arguments concerning education, Essa would allege, "You always said I could figure it out. You never said I could *do* it."

"Isn't it the same?" Nadine would ask vaguely.

Essa had long contended she would graduate from Wendell, the university on top of the mountain, but it wasn't locals who were accepted. The school attracted students from all over the country. "How will you possibly get in?" asked Nadine. Essa's high school counselors tended to push those who would actually go on to earn higher degrees to the community college at the bottom of the mountain instead, worried that the high school's unsophisticated graduates would not thrive at a school like Wendell attracting worldly youth who had grown up able to travel and saw their future in a place far beyond the mountains.

"It's an elite school," cautioned Nadine.

"It's a school school," answered Essa. "It's not elite. Plus, I know they'll take me," she said, spreading her fingers atop her head as if wearing a tiara. She suddenly breathed deeply and dramatically accepted an imaginary scholarship from an adoring audience, bowing in thanks.

Nadine had seen such antics before. "And how am I to pay for it?" she asked, striving to sound as logical as possible rather than betraying her financial anxiety.

Essa's school counselors had not broached the idea of a scholarship with her—or with others as a matter of fact. They had felt a certain anxiety themselves, worried that their students' academic failure in the wider world would reflect poorly on them. It was true. A child of the mountains might easily become overwhelmed at Wendell, perplexed by the workload while living away from home, for campus residency was required, and belittled by a student culture evincing more composure and intellectual finesse. Yet Essa's counselors seemed to forget that a student might also drink up the environment, latch on to youthful mentors whose newest delight in life might be to introduce a friend, very unlike themselves, to different views and ways of thinking.

However, to the counselors at Essa's school, it seemed much safer to encourage their more gifted students to attend the community college.

"Plus, you can sing," reminded Nadine. "Plenty do it." Nadine wanted Essa's life to be a melody.

"Plenty? Ma, name me some. You won't get beyond a handful. The whole idea sounds lovely but hardly practical."

"You can go record at that studio at the bottom of the mountain," Nadine suggested.

"That's a vanity place, Ma. It's just to make your own recording and then sell it yourself."

"Would that be hard? The selling part I mean."

At times like this Essa hardly knew how to discuss the outside world with her mother.

*   *   *

On one particular Saturday during this last summer before Essa began college, Nadine had been mashing baked sweet potatoes through a particular aluminum colander's rather generous holes to free them from lumps. A large bowl filled with the mounded mush sat on the counter in front of her. Lost in thought she stopped what she was doing, her back toward Essa who sat behind her at the kitchen table. She could not watch her daughter. The table's size was actually inadequate considering Essa's piles of brand new textbooks laying aside thick packages of ruled notebook paper and four three-ring binders of differing colors. Essa moved items here and there on the table's deeply scratched surface in silent contemplation, deliberating over her entrance to an academic world that excluded her mother. Nadine felt her daughter's unintentional ostracism keenly.

"I'll be so lonely in this place without you," Nadine lamented, feeling the meagerness of her small square of a kitchen. The warm oven to her left and the humming refrigerator to her right felt like cold comfort when considering Essa's adulthood. Nadine leaned forward to peer out the window in the back yard, her fingers gripping the edge of the porcelain sink. The window reflected a blank landscape.

"But I'll be back every night," reminded Essa. "I'm not moving there. It's a commuter school."

Nadine wiped her hands back and forth along her stomach, never without an apron when cooking. Today she wore one in faded purple tie dye that Essa had made a decade ago when her Girl Scout troop had been learning about the sixties. She moved a whisp of hair away from her face. Her hair had once been blond, but now seemed to be without color as she entered the second half of her life. Nadine shifted her weight and turned to face her daughter.

"I know, but you won't be here so regularly. I won't be able to count on you anymore. You'll have other obligations, meet other people—"

"Isn't that what college is for?" Essa asked, still staring at her various piles. "Aren't I supposed to gain independence? I'm supposed to learn to count on myself."

Essa put her hands to the sides of her head above her ears, open palms forward, her thumbs angled and almost hidden against her skull, index fingers touching. Eight fingers stood straight up in the air. "My crown," she said reassuringly.

Nadine smiled. When Essa had been small, she would create her crown when enjoying praise, her tiny hands forming the points of a certainly stunning though invisible tiara. Essa's bold self-presentation of a crown while walking across the stage at a ceremony to receive her award for academic excellence in the sixth grade had earned both mother and daughter the wrath of Essa's school principal.

"What sort of sign was she making?" Principal Tassanari asked, the mother and child by then in her office following the close of the assembly. The woman wore a creaseless gray wool suit, pointed heels, and a belt cinched tightly at the waist. "Is this one of those mountain things I'm supposed to be learning about? I haven't seen such bizarre behavior exhibited elsewhere."

"No," said Nadine quietly, both amused and annoyed. "It's just a thing we do."

"Do you realize what this sort of stunt could be signaling to the other students?"

Nadine unconsciously straightened her posture and elongated herself, becoming taller. "Do you mean that Essa is proud of herself? For that's all it meant, ma'am. If you see more in Essa's fingers than that, you're going to have to reconsider your own view, not Essa's."

The celebratory coronations had begun long ago when Nadine, economically unable to reward her daughter with any-thing but encouraging words, one day formed a crown with her own fingers and set it upon her daughter's head. Over the years the presentation had become more regal—but lasted never more than a moment before mother and daughter laughed. When pressed for time, Nadine was more apt to award her daughter an invisible star. "You may wear it all day," she would say impor-tantly, to which Essa would evince mock surprise and reply, "I am most certainly unworthy of this particular bequeathment."

Here in the kitchen Essa hardly looked like an adult to Na-dine. She wore simple jeans and a short, cropped orange shirt. Her bare feet lay crossed at the ankle underneath the table and her wild black hair was held tightly in a thick, cloth-covered elastic band.

"Ah, but you belong to this place," mused Nadine.

"Place is just space," remarked Essa offhandedly, stacking books.

"But this place is our home."

Nadine knew no one could touch her sweet potato muffins in flavor, and she guarded her secret as to why. Their sweet-ness was nonpareil. In the mid-afternoon she had retrieved the potatoes from their ash covering in the backyard. Here in the kitchen they had become cool enough to handle. Earlier, just after breakfast, she had gently scrubbed the sweet potatoes and wrapped them in foil, her ancestors having used discarded corn husks to accomplish the same task. She had also started a small wood fire in the backyard's elevated stone fire pit. (Her sister's husband, before he killed her in the shower, had built the pit, so he had been good for something Nadine conceded, though she did so ruefully and would never have admitted such a thing to anyone else.) After an hour the embers were hot and shimmer-ing. But instead of placing the potatoes on top of the elevated fire, Nadine would soon lay the wrapped sweet potatoes in a shallow nondescript hole some six inches deep into the ground next to the fire pit. The hole had been dug specifically and only for this purpose.

First she scooped the ashes from the fire pit with a small shovel and created a pillow of sorts at the bottom of the hole. One by one she dropped the potatoes softly into the depression. Small poofs of ash arose. Then she placed the fire pit's glowing embers in small groups on top of the potato pile. Two hours later she would use a soft brush to wipe away the black cinders, by then spent. If she didn't care about her eyes she might have simply blown away the feathery remnants they were so light and airy. Then from the hole she lifted out the most piquant of roasted sweet potatoes.

There are cooked sweet potatoes she thought, and then there are *mine*.

"This place is just space. Space is not a particular place," Essa continued.

Nadine disliked these circular discussions. She wished Essa showed more pride in their home. "But what do you call our home, our road, our community, young lady?" She turned back toward the bowl beside the sink and smashed the sweet potato mush in the colander unusually hard.

In a second bowl she had already mixed some of the potatoes with melted unsalted butter, always unsalted to maintain the sweetness of the potatoes, and then added eggs, flour and baking powder. The first pan of muffins was ready to emerge from the oven. Wick let her sell her muffins at Before You Go. He didn't even ask for a cut. They sold so well that he said he could never pay for such a great advertising draw. Nadine sold her muffins on no regular schedule, not wanting to be trapped into a baking cycle, so regular customers frequently asked about them, which gave her an immeasurable sense of pride. When she had the time she made a large basketful. It would be empty by the early afternoon.

"We have only the illusion of community here—" retorted Essa, but the oven's intruding, old-fashioned buzzer interrupted the completion of her latest thought. She too awaited the muffins.

Nadine bent over to open the oven's door, the heat assaulting her already sweaty face. She pulled the pan from the hot space with a gloved hand. Nadine's bakeware had been used for so many years and was so naturally greased that the muffins rolled out of their circled cups as soon as she turned the pan over onto a waiting towel laid out on the countertop to the right of the sink. From her chair Essa abandoned her cache of school supplies and sprinted to the counter to stand before the jumbled steaming tower.

"You know they should cool, little one," said Nadine. She enjoyed the fact that Essa, now a young adult, still could hardly wait for her muffins.

"Well, I'll help," she said laughing.

"You could have helped with the peeling and mashing some time ago, missy."

"Hm, help comes in many forms, Mama. I'll separate the pile for you so they can cool. See, aren't I helpful?"

As Essa "helped" with her left hand, poking and pushing the muffins apart from one another, but unable to touch one for long because of the intense internal heat, she also rather absent-mindedly searched for a specific cupboard's corner above with her right hand. When her fumbling fingers located the handle, she drew her eyes away from the muffins and pulled a small white Corelle plate from the bottom shelf. Nadine had bought the set of unsubstantial, lifeless plates based on their unbreakability after Essa's arrival, just as other budget-conscious mothers did. Choosing two muffins Essa determined to be the largest, she plopped them on the plate. She tore one in half knowing that using a knife would simply smash the overly hot gem. Butter already on the counter because of Nadine's baking, Essa took the knife laying crosswise on the tub's rim and scooped out a healthy dollop, smearing a great deal on each half of the open muffin. She picked up one section and sank her teeth into its moistness. The steam's heat was enough to burn the roof of her mouth, but over the years she had perfected a method of breathing in and out through her mouth, resulting in minor cooling all the while still eating—but sounding a bit like a chugging machine. In turn, however, some part of her body had to react to the scorching. Her eyes watered as a result.

"Now this is living." She chewed for a moment, the heat from her mouth rising into her nose. "You should sell these for a living."

Nadine could not suppress the well of emotion that sprang up within her. Only the sweat on her face disguised the tears moistening her own eyes. However, instead of saying what was in her heart, she spit out, "We can't live on muffins. You want me in a hot kitchen all day?"

"But back to the space thing, Mama," said an unperturbed Essa, ignoring the temporary sharpness in her mother's voice and continuing to chew. "Space is just what you occupy at any one time."

Nadine was disappointed to return to the space issue.

"But thanks to you I'm going on to occupy some new space down the mountain." Essa warmly hugged her mother. "And, man oh man, will I miss these," she said, indicating the muffins.

"Well, do like you like to do. I'm glad you're returning to this space each evening. I hope you'll still be around to eat one or two." Nadine said this firmly, regaining her composure all the while clutching her daughter so hard around the shoulders that Essa finally had to pull away.

And when customers were not plentiful and the store was quiet, Nadine thought of Essa, how she was becoming a woman and Nadine was losing her. She considered her daughter's mysterious history. She marveled that no one had come looking for her two decades ago, whoever she was at the time. Though she had been able to keep her for so long, Nadine worried about her daughter's identity, and the woman she would become. She had formed her, but who was she?

Essa had grown up in the mountains, yet could not pick out Joe-Pye weed along the road. She mistook goldenrod for ragweed and could walk straight into the middle of a poison ivy patch. Her ability to overlook Nature translated to an idiosyncratic consumption of Her bounty. Essa ate the tomatoes Nadine poached for her (Who eats unsalted *poached* tomatoes? wondered Nadine, though she prepared them b-a-r-e-l-y parboiled at her daughter's demand), and she dumped refrigerated cottage cheese over hot asparagus spears on a plate for lunch. She preferred to eat the kernels off a corncob raw, yet declined all offers of crisp, fresh fruit. Essa also rarely weighed the odds of any issue, leaping to a conclusion with great confidence from the start. "I'm going to cut my hair," she said one day without the usual agonizing female equivocation. "I'm looking too much like Victor's son Gale. Can't be looking like a primitive bushman."

But the proclamation that irked Nadine the most was Essa's periodic but insistent "I've been here before" when Nadine brought her to a place they clearly had never taken in. This line never failed to startle Nadine and then haunt her.

How much did Essa belong to her?

"I haven't changed my identity from what I was, Mama. I'm still that person. *And* I've added to it," Essa maintained.

Nadine felt stung. "But how could you have known who you were? You were too young."

"Somehow I was there, right in front of myself all the time," she said with a certainty Nadine did not like. "I just had to look."

Nadine wanted to close her eyes, to avoid seeing what Essa saw. But of course she was incapable of viewing the same panorama anyway. Her daughter's response had made Nadine profoundly sad. Essa could not stay home and sing. And soft sweet potato muffins made no one from Ethan a living.

.   .   .

Every morning Nadine rose from her bed and extracted herself from her mountain home to migrate along the back roads of Ethan. She navigated the route with ease until she surfaced at Highway 421, a strange kind of fountainhead, a realm of displacement at which Nadine felt both an urge to return home to avoid the intruding sense of dislocation as well as a compulsion to effect a necessary uprooting. *What is wrong with me?* Traveling from the sheltered haven of Ethan to the busy world of Before You Go, even though it was merely a gas station and convenience store, involved daily mental negotiation on Nadine's part. Sometimes she sat in her driveway at home a full ten minutes in the morning ... contemplating. Essa called it procrastination. Nadine called it preservation. Yet her shift between worlds never failed to happen in the same way, a result of her finally gunning the car's engine, as if the choice had really not been hers, to propel herself briefly up the mountain and make her usual appearance at the store.

Now at the end of her workday, Nadine sat in her car at the blacktop's edge between Before You Go's parking lot and 421. Though she might easily have pulled out, for the view up the mountain was far and relatively clear of vehicles, she waited for the widest gap possible. With barely a touch to the gas pedal, she began to roll down 421 at a mere ten miles an hour. As she gained momentum, she kept her foot from the pedal, letting gravity and the mountain's power pull her toward home. As the car's speed increased, she felt she had given over control. Decisions were no longer hers to make. Twenty ... thirty ... forty ... and then fifty read the speedometer's needle. The gauge reached sixty with her foot nowhere near the gas pedal, and she imagined sailing by Leaping Fork Road, the turn to Ethan, and continuing wildly down the mountain—to where she did not know. But before she knew it her foot instinctively moved to the brake and she found herself turning and driving herself back home.

COOPER RIDGE

It was a shortcut into town. She had driven *up* the curvy but
short mountain road many times. Never down. But this morning's routine had been unusual, not for its events, but because
she had ended up on the far side of town, so she thought for
once she would take Cooper Ridge to get back down the mountain to Slatyline Road. Slatyline was the flatter road which met
Cooper Ridge to create a T and, with a left turn, took you to the
nearest thing to a highway in the area.

Ascending Cooper Ridge one crawled, especially at the
hairpin turn when hugging the colossal rock to the right which
jutted out into the road. Nature did that, imposed itself, re-
minding one to stay alert. Today she wondered what the hairpin
turn would be like starting from above, the weight of the car
pressing her forward down the steep grade, toward the rock
and beyond.

For some reason the ride seemed exhilarating. She had just
bought, of all the unremarkable things in the world, a new toi-
letry bag for the trip to New Zealand. She looked forward to

pitching the old bag at home into the trash, torn in various spots from years of yanking at zippers and pulling open snaps. It currently sat ignored in a far corner of a bathroom cupboard, but she had always been practical enough not to throw something away before replacing it.

No one was on the road, behind her or climbing up. The elevation was some 500 feet from the top of Cooper Ridge to where it met with Slatyline below, so the car fell quickly, gathering momentum, and she stepped hard frequently on the brake to keep her speed in check. Halfway down she rounded the impressive rock, this time on her left, a new perspective. The day had turned gray, but the surroundings looked so unlike they usually did that she enjoyed them as though viewing a painting.

Cooper Ridge ended at Slatyline, but that didn't mean the road didn't continue. The county just gave it a new name: Green Briar. But on this day she didn't see the red stop sign. All she saw was the uninterrupted road ahead of her. She sailed right by the stop sign, the gray road blending in with the gray skies, crossed Slatyline, and suddenly found herself on Green Briar, almost floating up an incline, unknown houses with unknown inhabitants on either side of her.

By this time her foot was off the gas, letting the car coast. *Oh my, oh my, oh my, oh my* she repeated. The coasting hadn't seemed like her decision, just the sensation she was now experiencing. She remembered passing the stop sign, but only as a red flash. It hadn't registered as a warning. *Oh my, oh my, oh my, oh my.* How had it seemed so hidden? There had been no trees. Why had she seen Cooper Ridge as continuing rather than plainly recognizing the Slatyline Road intersection? Two whole roads crossing one another. Regulations specify a county road must be twenty-five feet wide. Who misses twenty-five feet of road space? And what if a car had been traveling on Slatyline, right at that time? And what if *two* cars—driving in each direction—had been traveling on Slatyline? And what if they had met to pass one another naturally, and legally, with plenty of room to spare, but she had been barreling down toward them? She had been traveling at most thirty-five miles per hour, but that would have been enough. Enough for ... *Slam*. And she working so hard on writing a book. It would not be published. And children. What if the cars had contained children? Unknown families. No matter the occupants, she would have created a human catastrophe.

It had been such a careless mistake, but here she was. She resolved to drive more carefully. But she had always been careful. She had never even been stopped by the police. Well, that wasn't true. She'd been involved in road blocks, that sort of thing, but all she did was show her license and registration before being waved on. She had had a parking ticket or two, and more than once she'd let the inspection sticker run out on the car. But who didn't commit that crime? And then once in California outside of Palm Springs she and her husband had been stopped in the middle of the highway, as had all the cars, by the immigration department. Were they harboring illegal aliens? How absurd she had thought at the time, but she and her husband politely complied with the official who simply scanned the interior cavity of their rental car. At the time the event had almost seemed exciting. She and Dan had both seen the signs depicting the silhouette of a fleeing adult clutching the hand of a tiny, pigtailed child. The child was suspended; its feet no longer seemed to hit the ground. Nothing like that happened in the mountains of North Carolina.

She spent the rest of the day on edge, the moment she had detected the unfamiliar surroundings beyond Slatyline imprisoned in her head. It became hard to let go of, to concentrate on her work. Once home she explained her foolishness to her husband, who, loving his wife, remained calm and didn't allow his fear at her oversight to show. And having told the story, and releasing the details and her own fears, she was able to forget the incident as one does a dream after waking.

She packed for New Zealand ...

And the next year she packed for Australia. And then China ... and then India. She and her husband ate well and gained too much weight. And in between trips she finished her self-help book, which did very well. Her publisher asked her to go on a speaking tour. And because she would be so publicly exposed, she resolved to lose the unwanted weight, which she was able to do remarkably quickly. She bought a new wardrobe. She appeared younger and spent a good deal of time in front of the mirror. Her husband teased her but in a gentle way. She knew most people were not so lucky. She resolved to include her approach to life, that when pain does occur, with a level head one might easily eradicate it, into her next book.

It was a smash.

.   .   .

Given the scene the two men emerged from the vehicle rather slowly. They stood glumly. One wore his street clothes; the other's shirt bore only the smallest indicator of help embroidered on his chest pocket, a snake, blood red, curling up a straight but nondescript dark rod. Such a curious insignia, almost foreboding. Once thought immune from sickness and disease, the snake had been viewed as a sacred creature until Hippocrates's teachings on rational medicine drew a line between logic and magic.

The rural road had not yet attracted cameras, and though a few onlookers had appeared—their quest not necessarily the source of the unexpected amplification but the subsequent silence—no one need shoo them away, for those who came too close recoiled, teetering.

Over to the men's left, the driver of their white van had turned off the vehicle's flashing lights, their mechanical desperation now seeming agonizing rather than precautionary.

"I heard all you see is gray, that some corner of the mind shelters the body from seeing and feeling its true predicament," said one.

"I heard you hover above, that you actually see your own body," said the other.

The first grimaced. "Not sure I'd want to see *that*," he said, pointing uselessly for there was nowhere else to look.

The men went dumb. The scene—the unfair encounter of flesh and steel—was so repulsive it would take time before its horror took root in the brain, drawing the necessary line between logic and magic.

THE AFFAIR

The school principal had arrived unannounced, as they all told her he would, during the middle of her second period fifty-minute literature class, quietly taking a seat in the back of the classroom. His posture implied he believed he could artfully do so—open a classroom door, scan the rows of desks, stride with tempered confidence right between them, and slide into an empty seat—all without causing any disruption; but only those with complete power are under this misconception of invisibility, and instead the entire tenor of the room changed instantly.

And yet every youthful face knew he was there to watch her, their teacher Katherine Murry, not them. The students' whole reason for sitting in those hard wooden chairs was to learn, to demonstrate later during exams and written critiques that they had absorbed classroom aims. And here *she* was the one being judged.

Arriving at school that morning she had discovered what looked to be a blank sheet of paper in her mailbox. She opened it to find a personal note—*HI KaTherine!*—scrawled in large, strangely formed letters of black ink across the unlined white page. She knew it had come from one of the younger maintenance men who was apparently infatuated with her. A few weeks ago she had asked him to fix a leg on the stool which sat before her podium, and now the man seemed, well, not stalking her really, but definitely too familiar. She had to be careful. People liked to talk, start rumors. Originally seeing the young man as a person pleasant enough to exchange good mornings with, she decided to avoid him. She crumpled up the piece of paper and dropped it into the recycling bin.

The morning had promised an extended moment of work time before classes began, but Katherine found them snatched from her instead, having to return a call to a testy parent, answer the department chair's questions concerning book numbers, eventually agreeing reluctantly to confirm the count in a particular supply closet as soon as she had a moment later in the day, and tabulate absences and tardies for the month of November after a secretary in the main office had again claimed her numbers were off.

While in the main office she waited in the public area for Principal Paul to finish a phone conversation. His personal secretary feigned interest in other duties but clearly kept an eye on her. The phone call over, Katherine hurried into Paul's office. He gestured toward the chair across from his desk but Katherine declined, simply asking his approval and signature for a club function. Though she had arrived with the proper paperwork, she was missing a section of numbers proving accountability—proper figures appearing properly on the proper lines. About to sign the document, Paul pulled his hand away, leaving it hovering strangely in the air. "Must remember the auditors," he said without meeting her eyes. Fifteen minutes later Katherine, by then wondering if she would arrive to her first period on time, obtained Paul's golden signature and rushed off to class.

Now in command of her eleventh grade American Literature class this early December morning she didn't need Principal
Paul's visit, yet she somehow maintained her composure, hoped
nothing in her facial muscles belied her annoyance, and continued her discussion of Walt Whitman's poems. Deftly, she felt,
she compared the poet's striking early modern presentation,
his references to sexuality, electricity, and feverish explora-
tion—far too early for the actual literary Modern Era that was
not to come until decades later, she explained—to the changes
wrought by war protesters and hippies in the sixties. Was Dr.
Paul seeing evidence of her historical connections and careful
planning? Did he know enough about Whitman himself to understand the analogies?

Was he bored to death?

She poured four years of undergraduate study and two
years of graduate work into her presentation, and for a moment at the lecture's end, she hoped for student applause. Of
course it didn't come. This was high school after all. But what
if they had applauded her? Stood up from their confining desks,
come to the point of, say, serenading her, right in front of him,
he who had come unannounced and wielding such an air of
intimidation?

Instead, she handed back a graded ten-question quiz ad-
ministered the previous day. Momentarily each student sat
hunched over his or her individual answer sheet as though reading the day's fortune. Katherine gave her class a moment with
their work and then spoke, her sharp voice cracking through
the air, alarming many. She reminded them appropriately of
their homework, and then the bell rang. *Perfect timing.* From
her desk she watched her students file out the door, some more
animated now, others still feeling the presence of the principal.

And then *he* stopped before her desk—not the principal
but her problem, the student who throughout the semester had
always found an excuse to erase the need to fulfill his next class
obligation.

"You marked one of my answers wrong on the quiz," he claimed, "and it's right." He stood before her desk, arms hanging at his sides, looking as lazy as one could while still remaining upright. His shaggy hair burst wildly out of his scalp and then fell at all angles, nearly obscuring his eyes. He didn't reach to flick any strands away. A direct look into his teacher's eyes was not his intent.

The principal still sat in his chosen place in the last row of desks against the back wall. The room was wide but shallow so he was just six desks away, straight in front of her, Katherine, his new employee, his project. Had she looked over either of her student's puny, underdeveloped shoulders, her gaze would have landed directly on the man. Yet he did not appear to be listening.

Katherine took the offered sheet from her student. If he was correct, he would pass the quiz, earning a seventy percent instead of a sixty percent. She stood behind her desk, he in front of it, three horizontal feet of wood keeping them apart. True or False had been the only answers possible.

Before administering any quiz, Katherine always reminded her students to write out the words True and False, not to use the capital letters T and F, which could easily be mistaken for one another depending on one's handwriting. But this student had not listened. He had used letters. The previous night while home grading, she had decided to overlook the fact that he had not followed directions. She had not marked the paper with a zero as she had threatened to do during class. She hadn't wanted to discourage this student, turn him away even more from his studies. It was early December and she had the rest of the school year to put up with him after all.

But Katherine had also made it a habit to grade each quiz twice, making certain she had not marked a correct answer as incorrect. So at this moment it was highly unlikely she had made a mistake. She simply didn't.

She looked more closely at the boy's answers. The letters T and F could look just the same when written by hand depending on the sort of decorative emphasis one cared to take with the "roof" of the T and the "arm" of an F. And then there was just plain sloppiness of course. Hence, the only difference could be the short lower line. Was it present for an F or absent for a T?

And there it was.

The area under the T's cross on her student's quiz was circled in green pen, the color she used for grading, meaning she had noted the small line's absence last night at home. Yet her student had written in, *just moments ago*, right while the principal was in the room, the small line to make his T look like an F.

She clenched the page creating a diagonal crease.

In a voice barely above a murmur, she firmly explained her circling process to her student with two terse statements. He stared straight into her face, undeterred. In response, Katherine kept her eyes bored into his. She would not look above her shoulders to meet the eyes of the principal six desks away who, instead, was scanning the room's bulletin boards of student work and school announcements. She would not let him know that this conversation was anything but an opportunity to help, to answer a student's question.

"Do you realize what a position you have put each of us in at this moment?" she hissed.

The boy stood still, waiting to see how she would handle the situation. He had been in trouble plenty of times before.

"Do you realize that I could turn you around and explain to the principal right now what you have done?"

The boy stood passively.

"If you *ever* try this again …"

She placed the quiz on the surface of her desk and wrote "No Credit" at the top of the page. Having originally earned a sixty, her student would now earn a zero. And then she added the word "Cheated." Had she been home grading during the evening, she would have written the words darkly, heavily, with a flourish. And then she would have underlined them. But here in the classroom with its buzzing fluorescent lights, the uncaring boy before her, and the reason for her teaching position patiently awaiting the conclusion of what he must have mistakenly perceived as a Positive Teaching Moment, she folded her arms to her chest, her student's quiz yet in her hand, the gesture demonstrating the page was now hers.

"I will keep this. You are to go."

Without changing his expression, the boy left the room. He had acknowledged neither his act nor Principal Paul's presence.

Finally Paul rose, unfolding his large body from the tight space. "Glad to see a bit of conversation with students following class. I'm sure he appreciated it, Katherine. That one, he can be a bit of trouble as I'm sure you're aware."

Katherine manufactured what she thought was a smile, but had someone taken a photograph of her at that moment, she would have seen that her lips remained quite straight and thin.

"I'll write up my notes and we can set up a meeting," he said somewhat wearily, all the while heading for the door. "Thanks for having me."

And then he was gone.

Katherine collapsed into her desk chair. It was not yet 10 A.M. She still had another four classes to teach, a meeting to attend during her duty hour, another signature yet to obtain from the principal himself—*groan*—and After-School Exterior Management to perform, a lofty name invented by administration for old-fashioned bus duty—without busses, of course, here in the city.

·   ·   ·

And yet the day ended well. Her students had been prepared and attentive. At 3:10 P.M., the final bell having rung, she turned off the lights to her classroom, shut the door tightly, and briskly walked down the hall to the English department's work room where she yanked her coat and hat off a peg, one of the many protruding in a neat line stretching across the three walls of a back closet. She fished around somewhat desperately in her deep pockets, finally locating her mittens. Her colleagues, just returning from their own classrooms, felt her plight. After-School Exterior Management was high on no one's list. Only brief greetings and half smiles were exchanged, both in the English department work room and the hallways, as she dashed toward the school's main entrance. She never enjoyed this pace, racing to be present on the sidewalk at street level two stories below before as many of the released students she was supposed to be "managing," loud and loose-lipped by this time, had arrived.

Back in the work room a man in a long and elegant dark coat loomed in the doorway asking for Katherine. She didn't know he was coming he told the dozen or so teachers. The women of the room, formerly purposeful in their activities but now taken aback, twittered. She was just here they chorused, as though Katherine's absence were a serious concern.

Was she finished yet he wondered.

By this time two women had vacated their desk chairs and were moving toward the man as though he were magnetic. The male teachers in the room marveled at the man's presence as well. He was tall and square and could have walked off the pages of a fashion magazine. As the man apologized for the interruption, the group caught glimpses of his tailored suit beneath his coat. The movement of the two women gravitating toward him was arrested. He removed his leather gloves which he then stroked with his hands. This was not a gesture of arrogance, at least as perceived by the women. Later, the two who had attempted to mesh their presence temporarily with his, would call him dashing.

As the minutes wore on and the man waited patiently, the other women in the room felt paralyzed at their individual desk stations against the walls, as though the man were allowed free reign while they were tethered to the room's perimeter. They whispered, their eyes darting around the room, landing on the man when they could afford to do so without looking silly.

How could he show up *here*? Their men never did.

The male teachers soon tired of the atmosphere of restraint and went back to their textbooks and stacks of papers. Finally the boldest of the women found new reason to fawn, offering Katherine's beau a chair, then coffee, and then, at a loss for what else of herself to give, returned to her work, unable to focus on the closing details of the day. They knew so little about her, this Katherine who had taken the eleventh grade position just two days before the semester's onset.

"Ah, you're *here*," cried Katherine when she re-entered the work room some twenty minutes later. Her fellow instructors noticed her flushed cheeks and wondered whether the afternoon's cold or the presence of the striking man had caused the color.

"Thought I needed two signatures today from Dr. Paul, but I needed a third as well," she explained without stopping and to no one in particular. The principal intimidated her but she'd get used to him. "That's what took an extra minute." She gathered up her book bag, swung its strap over her shoulder, and left with the magnificent man. Was she moving so quickly on purpose? Was she trying to let her colleagues see as little of him as possible?

.   .   .

He was nearly a foot taller than she, but they walked in unison, each with an arm around the other's waist, further into the city, leaving the school building behind. It was just after 4 P.M. A light snow had fallen, enhancing the twinkle of the lights now combating the growing dimness of a winter's late afternoon.

"You looked lovelier than ever when I first saw you as you rushed in after ... what is it called?"

"After-School Exterior Management."

"What a name." He squeezed her firmly, practically lifting her off the sidewalk sideways.

Katherine let out a happy squeal.

"I thought you'd be done closer to 3:15."

"Ah, I'm learning. No matter what your past teaching experience is, first-year people end up on loads of committees. Do your initial duty, I've found, and later you can say no. Plus, I now know nothing gets done around there without Principal Paul's signature."

They window shopped. They forgot the day and its obligations. From the store's displays they chose items for one another, presented imaginary gifts. They stood in front of a travel agency and planned a trip to Australia.

"We couldn't," she sighed.

"Why not?"

The moving street crowd both isolated and insulated them, made up of eager shoppers as well as individuals more intent on returning home than absorbing the beckoning consumer Christmas pageant. Katherine's hair glistened, even blazed, in the city's lights. Tumbling onto the thick scarf wrapped twice around her neck, her curls, now raised, framed her face in a way the man found both childlike and alluring. She looked into his eyes, feeling his command, and had no qualms about letting him control the evening.

"*Here.*" He guided her into an Indian restaurant, the closing door behind them instantly shutting out the bustle of the sidewalk.

"What about ... ? But her words were no form of resistance. "It's so early," she said without force.

For a moment, but only a moment, she thought about the dinner for two she had left defrosting on the small kitchen counter inside the two-room apartment on Park Slope, just a 357-square foot space but with a wide bay window in front and a separate bedroom in back, intimate and whisper-private and tucked away from the city's shouts and complaints.

The waiter would lead them to his best table he said, gesturing to the two chairs surrounding a small café table in a front window's alcove. "You may watch life go by while you relax here."

"Oh ... no." Katherine saw just a thin pane of glass between herself and the clusters of people on the sidewalk. "My stu—"

"A darker corner, please," requested the man. His even voice calmed Katherine.

"I understand," said the waiter. He was a professional. He took no offense. His aim was to please every customer in every way. As if silently acquiescing to join a conspiracy, he led the man and woman to a booth nearer to the kitchen but one offering privacy and peace.

They each ordered a curry, hers Malai Kofta, *mild please*, potatoes and homemade cheese simmering in cashews and a cream sauce. His was Butter Chicken, *medium*, cooked with tomatoes into a seasoned pungency, giving him the bite he expected. Once the words had left their mouths it was already delicious to anticipate the coming tastes. They would also share the spicy, potato-filled Amritsari Kulcha, he told the waiter, after Katherine had pointed to it from the menu's list of nans.

"See, I'm adventurous too," she reminded him. She lowered her eyes to spread her napkin over her lap, but she suppressed a smile.

"I'm well aware of that."

"I know you are."

An hour later, after tearing the kulcha into ragged pieces and purging each silver serving bowl of its vegetables, meats, and nuts, the sauces' remainders of complimentary crimsons, still glistening in the bowls' depths, proved too savory to abandon. They secretly conspired to mix the thick sauces, her mild, his spicier, wondering how loudly the chef would object were he to discover them.

Katherine carefully scraped the remnants of her bowl into a takeaway container, and then licked the spoon she had used before laying it squarely across her plate. Her partner then cupped his bowl aloft, almost menacingly so, until he smiled. He tipped his bowl, the head of the stream plunging down, its impact parting the scarlet brown sauce into two lips which rose to embrace its entry.

"Together they might explode," he said slyly. His eyes shot fire as they landed on Katherine.

"Or"—her eyes did not leave his—"they could make for an interesting breakfast."

They exited the restaurant and continued walking the city streets, now slowly, he holding the small container of what they had together created. Inside, the contents smoldered. The two strolled in silence, having melted into one another.

"Katherine, let's pretend we're not married and duck into a hotel," he suggested excitedly.

"But the dinner we were supposed to ... it's on the counter ... overnight it ..."

"Let it spoil. Let's not spoil this."

Katherine loved him deeply.

And they turned into the Chinta Ria Hotel.

. . .

At Hunter Slope High School the next morning the academic day began quite routinely. Within its administrative environs, however, some business had come to a head.

"She's always in there," said Principal Paul's personal secretary, "hiding out in the mailroom just to be near *his* office."

"Twice just yesterday," confirmed the bookkeeper, who had her own office down the hall and really should not even have been able to notice Katherine's comings and goings.

"No, *three* times," corrected a part-time secretary. "After classes were over yesterday I saw her go in there *again*."

The women who worked in the front office of Hunter Slope created a beehive of voices. They whispered of the affair Katherine was surely having with Principal Paul.

ZERO O'CLOCK ON
THE TENTH OF NOTHING

It had started with the clock, an atomic clock that was supposed to know what to do, formulated in some magic way to understand time and space in order to calculate the exact time and day anywhere on Earth through interaction with the stars or planets, or maybe both. It even vowed to keep up with daylight savings time, mankind's desperate eternal desire to control time's passage.

But the clock didn't work, refusing to conform to the mechanism's instructions right there *as written on the box* which housed it upon its arrival: "This clock will adapt to and coincide with current attitudes toward daylight savings time." *Current attitudes?* Well, what kind of attitude was *zero* o'clock? On this lovely fall morning where the enormous three-inch numbers should have exhibited the time, with the little colon flashing as though bravely keeping the digits of the hour and minutes safely separate from one another, the clock's display had been blank. Left was a boring gray space. Below where the time should have appeared, the second line of information—the month, name of the day, moon phase, and temperature—had vanished as well. The only remaining evidence of the clock's prior mission had been retained in the cramped half-inch space meant for the date. Two digits, a one and a zero, were the only presence in the gray gloom. Hence, the day had become the 10th of Nothing.

Despite the day's absenteeism on the time piece, as her husband called the atomic clock, as though it were a glittery watch bought from a jeweler, the day's work was real. And she had become tired of her neighbor's sideways looks from across the road. Yes, she had been running the leaf blower on and off for three hours, but it was the weekend. *When else would you like me to complete this job, Josie?* In addition, because the machine's bright orange extension cord had to make its way down the hundred-foot driveway, including negotiating its big curve around a giant rock, it kept unplugging from the Hurricane 560. **RrrrOOORRR** for ten minutes and then the machine would cut out, its cord deciding to wrap around her ankle or become stuck on a jutting angle exposed in the confusion of rip rap rocks aiding the drainage to the driveway's side. It would snap out of the 560 causing a pronounced silence and a corresponding deafening fury within Carmen's head. Repeatedly she unwound the cord from around her boots or used the same boots to clomp angrily toward the place where it had decided to hug a rock's edge. Adding to her aggravation, she could hardly see for all the dust and debris in the air.

And then **RrrrOOORRR** once more, but only until the cord separated yet again from the machine.

Her arms were tired but her legs hurt too. Why had she listened to the stupid woman on the television who suggested that for all these years, four decades for Carmen herself, that she had been shaving her legs in the wrong direction. She was to shave *down* her leg, not up. And so yesterday she had made the change, resulting in more little blood dots on her leg than she could count, each angry follicle now marking its presence.

And then just hours later she had to go and do something like crash her left shin into the dishwasher door, which had been hanging open to the floor. She could blame no one; just walked right into the thing, as though she was new to the kitchen, her own kitchen of twenty-five years, creating two bloody gouges where the corners of the door met greedily with her flesh.

Her whole body ached.

And her husband Tim? *Inside.*

Tim. Who named a child Tim? Not Timothy. Just Tim. Not even called Timmy as a child. Just her husband *Tim. Together Tim. Tidy Tim. Thrifty Tim. Even Teetotaler Tim.* Always cool, always dressed well, always trim. Yup, *Trim Tim.* So many admirable qualities, but they weren't doing her any good at the moment. Right now he was up there in the living room, just beyond the window which she could see from the bottom of the driveway, watching TV and nursing that cracked rib of his. It may as well have been a rack of ribs because he was useless after a fall from his mountain bike—"maintaining health" he called it while she was deteriorating. "You should try riding, Carmi," he would say. He called her Carmi when he wanted to be doting—or was it that he wanted to be serious? Because he would look at her, a hard stare, or at least a stare that felt too heavy, too accusatory. Well, her deteriorating self didn't want to ride any mountain bike while these leaves needed extraction from all the drainage ditches on their property. Damn the mountains and their beauty. In Mother Nature's world water only ran one way, *down.* And drainage ditches don't work when clogged with tens of thousands of brown leaves pasted in the form of thick gooey mats to the myriad angles presented by rip rap rocks.

And now she realized her arms hurt like hell, holding the Hurricane 560, sending leaves into a wild, violent whoosh before her, the whole collection of which evinced only the slightest notion of direction. Their recklessness required her to move from side to side in a vain effort to contain the widening ends of a giant unruly leaf triangle, her eyes concentrating like a dancer on an invisible point, only this one a continually shifting destination twenty feet ahead.

And she knew Tim was up there watching that stupid Asian show *Japanizi—Going, Going, Gone*. The only glimpse of an episode she had ever caught involved giant carp lying on tables displayed before little children dressed as fishermen in colorful plastic garb, all mimicking the man on the Gorton's frozen fish box. The host of the show ran around the stage, periodically speaking into a microphone as though spilling secrets. *This was fodder for Thinker Tim?* Besides, he should have been out taking care of the hornets in the wall, a whole group of them—A *buzz?* Were they called a *buzz?*, or maybe a *ring*, or was it a *hum* of hornets? Animal groups always had weird names. They were currently trying to make a hive in the back corner of the house, *in* the wall. Someone with cracked ribs was capable of walking, right? But he wouldn't listen. *Inattentive Tim.* A couple of days ago she had put a piece of masking tape over the hole, feeling smug while watching the hornets gather, their anger clearly rising; however, on her next check just a half an hour later she found the insects flying in a kind of hover, creating a hazy hornet mist before the hole they'd created, greedily eating through the tape.

Tomorrow. He could be that too, *Tomorrow Tim*. "Put it on my list, Carmi." He was always coming up with ridiculous deductions: "Did you know if Erica Hill from NBC married Captain America she'd be Erica America? Say it, Carmi, *Er-ica A-mer-ica*." Such a star he was on campus with his students, every lecture fit for print. Well, those students should hear him at home. Erica America. Give me a break. No, make *me* a star too. I could handle that, figured Carmen.

But he should get up. He should be *Transformation Tim*, ignoring his rib pain and actively participating in whatever she presented to him. After all, he was the one who stayed so damn healthy.

She herself felt she had turned doughy and lumpy, her stomach like the unformed protrusion of a baking pie, deciding to bubble here first, and now there. Only it wasn't a stomach. Stomach implied a necessary organ—like that of *Tight Tim*. Instead, she contended with a *belly* which she pushed into her pants each morning. Tim called her beautiful and worked in vain to convince her she was too hard on herself. "Five foot eight at 140, Carmi?" What did she have to complain about? But to herself she was *Chubby Carmen, Chunky Carmen*. She knew it from the mirror.

As a child she and her best friend had looked for the diamonds between their legs. On TV, or maybe it was in some teen magazine, they had learned that perfectly formed lower limbs manifested two diamonds. All one had to do was stand with the sun behind to create a shadow; there on the sidewalk's concrete two perfectly proportioned diamonds would reveal themselves, one between the thighs and knees and the other below the knees to the ankles. To Carmen and her best friend these areas were nebulous, their mining for the lines of calculated gemology proving fruitless given the squishy adolescence of their bodies. They already felt flawed and incomplete at ten years old.

Carmen took in one last scowl from Josie, who still stood in her front yard striving to maintain an intimidating presence, and then began the arduous trip back up the driveway, requiring her to bend over to make periodic stops to pick up reasonable sections of the hundred feet of electrical cord, all the while balancing the Hurricane 560. *And why 560? Was it better than a 550? Where did manufacturers derive these numbers from?* She wrapped the thick, heavy line around her left arm, and when the loops became too unwieldy she simply dragged the rest of the cord behind her, dropping the entire mess at the base of her Ford Explorer sitting to the right of her husband's more modest—at least in size—Prius at the top of the driveway. Both vehicles were pointed toward the door of the two-car garage, somehow never making it into the garage itself. *Please clean out the garage one of these days, Tim.* Such a collection of journals and scholarly stuff. Why couldn't it be kept on campus?

Tender Tim, that being tender in the rib, lay on the couch reading his latest find in the world of economics, the television off. She couldn't even complain. *Theorist Tim.*

"I'm off to run errands. Need anything?"

"I'm good," he said, laughing, *Tickled Tim,* at something he read on the page. *Who laughs at economics?*

On the way out Carmen managed to back over the wadded up hundred-foot cord she had left behind her car. At least the Hurricane 560 had been deposited safely to the side. She rubbed her left elbow, the jostling over the messy bundle of orange line having knocked her into the driver's side door.

Sometimes while she drove the days had names, and today was Pull-in-Front-of-Carmen Day. She lowered her head into her shoulders as they rose to lessen the length of her neck. She didn't know why this position made her feel better but it did. *Cross Carmen.* She gripped the steering wheel as she approached the next curve. Hard to be *Charitable Carmen*, especially when the windshield needed such a cleaning. Tim had mentioned its condition just the other day. So why hadn't *he* found some paper towels and the bottle of Windex. And afterward moved right into the garage toward those darn journals.

And then there he was.

Dalanzo!

Hardly checking the rearview mirror she pulled to the left, now halfway into the next lane, careening along—legally—at 50 mph. Had a car been in her blind spot she would have smashed into it.

Dalanzo. *Dimwitted Dalanzo. Dumb Delanzo.* He walked around town with those earplugs in his ears listening to who knows what and disregarding the rules of life. At least someone had cautioned him to walk facing traffic. Of course he couldn't have a license, something was wrong with him, but Carmen didn't know what. She just didn't want to be the one to drive a car over him. *Carnage Carmen.*

The post office, she just needed to get to the post office; after that she promised to inch herself around town from errand to errand. *Competent Carmen. Capable Carmen.* She would happily put up with whoever wanted to be in whatever lane. Well, maybe.

.   .   .

The papers later called her courageous, *Courageous Carmen,* and CNN even described her as compelling, *Compelling Carmen,* since the burglar clearly noticed her presence. Just look at the video.

It was said he knew what he wanted, boldly walking through the lobby just as Carmen had, practically *with* Carmen excited neighbors pointed out. He strode toward concealed locked doors to the packages behind, to areas the public never sees, clearly intent on his aim. An inside job most townies surmised, wondering how close they might be to those involved. And thank goodness Carmen had left the building and already exited the parking lot when the explosion occurred. What might have happened? Some speculated on more than luck—a pure psychic experience. *Cosmic Carmen.* Still, Carmen finally became a star.

It turned out that Carmen's public life ended, on tape at least, at 2:05 pm. The video went on for another twenty-six seconds, and included the criminal's long look at Carmen, but it ended with his seeming evaporation just before the explosion.

She had simply been on camera as the lone visitor to the post office lobby at that moment that afternoon, shoving her mail, three bills and their payments, into the slot with a certain firmness, something remarked on by the media because the next so-called patron turned burglar, had looked so wary. Carmen, however, later enjoyed every viewing she caught of herself on television, how good she looked from above—long trim legs and a new fleece jacket that seemed to accentuate her waist rather than expand it. If only she could be viewed from a ceiling camera at all times.

The explosion had been calculated, as determined by the town police and later the FBI, but Carmen knew no details. They were fuzzy and she really didn't care; however, though Carmen's involvement ended with her exit from the security camera's view, for the town the story only *started* with her disappearance from the camera's reach.

Yes, the police had questioned her, but she had noticed no other car in the parking lot or human in the lobby. She had heard no sounds worthy of recall and seen nothing amiss in what she remembered of the lobby's space. The police had thanked her for her time and quickly dismissed her.

For an extended moment, however, she was the main attraction in town. No more *Common Carmen*. Friends called, people recognized her and stopped her on Main Street, and one restaurant owner brought her a copy of the day's paper and offered her a free dessert, which she happily accepted, though Tim frowned. *Typical Tim*. She tapped the front page to show who was important. Her name looked good in a headline. She grinned to show Tim she was kidding. At least that's what she told herself she was doing.

In their excitement news junkies peppered her with questions, always the same ones: "What had he looked like?" "Was he a townie or an outsider?" And because no one had died, a few even romanticized him: "Had he been good looking?" And even the ridiculous was asked: "Would she sue for pain and suffering after the trial?"

Trial? *What trial?*

Instead, Carmen fed herself on the constant portrayal of her personage, caught at an angle which resulted in a slimmer version of herself, the self she imagined being if only she knew how.

But with fame being a fleeting companion, within a few days she realized her life had ended at 2:05 that afternoon when she disappeared through the post office's doors and off the screen, back to her normal existence.

She had enjoyed the attention. Left behind had been the prodding of her husband, cleaning leaf bits from her eyes, stumbling around yard obstacles, and avoiding hornet companionship.

Her celebrity faded and closed, every day again like the 10th of Nothing.

.   .   .

A few weeks later the weather had turned bitter, compounded by a biting wind and the occasional swirl of flurries. As she drove into town she saw him again, Dalanzo, at nearly the same point in the road's curve, facing oncoming traffic, only this time he was pushing a rickety old-fashioned bike up the long hill. His thin coat remained unzipped and he wore no mittens or hat. He stopped to press each hand to his face, one at a time, balancing the old bike with the other. As she was wont to do, Carmen lowered her head into her shoulders, letting her shoulders rise. She groaned. *Why did this guy have to hang around town? Where did he even live?* She wanted to hide, pretend she didn't see him.

But *Conscientious Carmen* emerged. She would do something for him and then be done with it. But there was no real compassion involved; it was her own guilt she wanted to assuage.

As soon as she could safely do so, Carmen made a left and swung the car around into the opposite lanes, circling back up the road, past Dalanzo, and then made another left at the top of the hill, slowly making her way toward the man, stopping before him on the shoulder. He was of indeterminate age and evinced no facial expression or even recognition of the monstrous Ford SUV before him. In fact, he simply shifted his location so as to move around Carmen and her car. Clearly he was used to navigating through a world that did not recognize him.

Carmen reached over to her glove compartment and while fumbling within its interior she called out to Delanzo before she had even rolled down her driver's side window. In fact, in her exuberance she successfully shouted only to her passenger side floor mat. *Crazy Carmen.*

Naturally the man hardly noticed.

Carmen righted herself and with her left index finger clumsily mashed down the proper lever on the door to lower her driver's side window. Somehow without thinking the extra set of mittens she kept in the glove compartment were deftly transferred from her right hand to her left hand in order to dangle them as close as she could get them to Dalanzo's body.

"Please take these."

Dalanzo stared not at Carmen but at the mittens. Carmen fairly held her breath as the wind jettisoned itself with abandon into her face and within the car, swiftly sweeping out its heat. Outside Dalanzo seemed strangely unaffected, his focus on the mittens.

She could only see half of the man's face, but slowly his grimace seemed to relax and he took the mittens, gently, not as she expected, in some sort of snatch. Yet he was silent, his facial response, like any words he might have spoken, hardened and stolen by the wind.

You might thank me you demented soul.

As far as she knew he had not looked her in the face. He simply moved on, and even using the side-view mirror, she could not tell if he had stretched the mittens onto his hands.

With little left to do, Carmen moved the gear shift into Drive and let the vehicle start rolling forward. Realizing the strikes of wind were still hitting her, she lightly pulled the window's lever up. The window did not respond. She stopped the car and jerked the lever again, harder and this time with two fingers. The window remained inert. She gripped the window's top edge with her right hand, tugging with some force, now pawing erratically and inefficiently at the lever with her left hand. The glass was so cold. And then she abandoned the lever and used both hands at the window. Her eyes stung. Delanzo had merely walked away, to where she did not know.

Later that day it would cost her $256 to have the window's mechanism repaired. Her bank account held substantial funds and she would write the check using warm nimble fingers.

Until then she turned to the spit and spite of Nature's assault entering at will through the car's window. Each sting cut an edge of Delanzo's existence into her flesh. He carries his world with him wherever he is, she realized.

She did as well and she knew the question should become how. *Carmen's clarity.*

THE DOOR

To Leonida, Heaven would be accessible through a door, no permeable grand gate, which she felt a stern God would not permit. You were either in or you were out. Her daughter Bindy asked whether there would be angels dressed in white, sporting filmy wings like children dressed up on Halloween. Leonida threw her shoulders back and, overlooking her daughter's mocking tone, stood firm. The wings would be structured and functional, she thought, not for flying exactly, but likely for hovering and floating. In fact, Leonida had contemplated Heaven's environment a great deal. The air would be pure, almost like that of breathing through an oxygen mask, which she had experienced one summer after a bad fall which had injured her back when Bindy was a teenager; in addition, she would be forever without the sweat of life. Never again would she encounter an employer's dirty dish or soiled garment to wash. However, concerning the stability of Heaven's clouds as a kind of floor, Leonida was less sure. She imagined a series of wood planks, visually vast and widely strewn in some sort of godly but systematic manner. To Bindy, the idea of planks, as her mother termed them, only conjured up Emily Dickinson's planks of reason, which "broke" as Dickinson's speaker "dropped down, and down."

Bindy was only vaguely ethnic, both by choice and default as her mother would never clarify her own origins. Leonida's preface to most any statement was "In my country ...," but she never specified a location. Her mother spoke mostly German, but claimed it wasn't her native tongue; in addition, she had adopted idioms of the Eastern European women of her neighborhood, but, Bindy suspected, only in an effort to fit in. To her, Leonida's name felt Italian, with her own name more tied to India, yet her mother sometimes spoke of her homeland's cold tundra as though having lived in Russia's Siberia. Bindy's pointed questions brought only vague answers from Leonida: "The boundaries changed after World War II," she would half explain, or "Where I grew up has vanished." At other times she would simply dismiss Bindy's queries with "Such places don't exist in the modern world: *Hätte ich hundert Jahren würdest du doch gar nichts verstehen.* "If I had a hundred years you still couldn't understand." But whatever the place had been, its beliefs and practices lived within Leonida's fingertips and daily had been brushed brusquely onto Bindy during her childhood, and from her mother's lips snapped lines that would haunt her daughter long after her mother's death.

Bindy's father described his wife as "so determined she would walk through a wall." And that was about all he had ever said. He and Bindy had rarely talked directly, moving around one another as orbiting satellites within their tiny New York tenement apartment. Yet, one day for no reason Bindy could now recall, her father took her for a whole day's adventure to Coney Island. It was 1947 and she had been fourteen. This event remained singular until five years later in a church when he would touch her shoulders and lean forward to bestow upon her forehead the only kiss he would ever release to her—just before he turned her toward the groom.

Instead of being excited about the Coney Island trip, she had spent the hours prior to their departure anticipating what she should talk about. Years later, with children of her own, she realized she had put the burden of communication on herself, as though she alone had been responsible for the outing's success, forgetting that her father should participate as well. But they did not talk. A whole subway ride to and from Coney Island, as well as an afternoon in between absorbed in a carnival-like atmosphere, produced not a word she could remember. Now she wondered how that could have been, but at the time the silence had seemed normal.

The night Leonida left Bindy's house for the last time in the winter of 1976 she slammed the door in anger, awakening her sleeping daughter on the second floor. Now as a contemplative adult, Bindy knew her mother had spent a lifetime deceiving herself, telling Bindy stories she knew weren't true, indulging in fairy tales that grew in her mother's own sense of credulity with each version. Gravely, Leonida swore that as a small child she had been snatched away by gypsies from the railroad tracks. Another time it was the government. But what would the government have wanted with a child? She also pictured her mother as a lone toddler sitting on a rail, no one in sight, which was ridiculous, not only as an image but also because her mother had been the last of thirteen children. Some older sibling, given parental charge, must have been in the vicinity. Another story had the family descending from aristocrats, though Leonida had reworked this story to focus on herself as well. As she told it, *she*, not necessarily the family, descended from a duchess. Bindy concluded this detail might have originated with a kind father, Bindy's own grandfather whom she had never met, to add light to his daughter's life. Or, Bindy had to admit, maybe it was because Leonida had been her grandparents' pearl at the end of raising the first dozen children in an old world long forgotten.

Bindy knew she had not been wanted, or at least the original intent of her presence had been lost to her parents. Her father and mother would argue in the tiny Upper East Side kitchen: "You wanted a child." "No, *you* wanted a child." The speakers were interchangeable. The thin wall between the kitchen and Bindy's bedroom kept out none of the pain. Nevertheless, Leonida offered her daughter the experiences of a modern American life—gymnastics, swimming, camp—because, as Bindy rationalized, the opportunities for Leonida had not existed. But her mother would never have admitted so. Inquiries into the conditions of her mother's childhood meant that Bindy was questioning her own privileges, showing her ingratitude.

"You're being snotty," Leonida would say and the conversation would be closed.

Du weist gar nichts. While Bindy was told she "knew nothing," Leonida professed to know a great deal. She even knew Death, for one night she had seen him enter through the apartment door. In that instant she had understood someone would die, but she didn't think it would be Papa. It had happened in 1956 but years later she still saw Death plain as day in her mind. After dinner Bindy's father had retreated to the back bedroom to smoke a cigarette. Her parents did not sleep together and they hadn't as long as she could remember. He had emitted an odd noise, which Leonida plainly heard from the kitchen in the compact space of four cramped rooms, calling from the kitchen, "Plagued by the *dybbuk*, Papa? Don't be silly."

He would do that, pretend he was needy in a dramatically distracting way, pulling her away from her work just for attention. Still she went to him.

Moments later she ran down the five flights of stairs to the police station across East 126th Street and, dry-eyed, told the officer on desk duty, "My husband just died."

He had smoked the equivalent of two packs of cigarettes a day and was a functional alcoholic. Bindy was quite familiar with the local bars since her father frequently sent her down the street to Andy's Place for four cigarettes, which you could buy loose in those days. Her father would simply point. If he spoke to his daughter at all he did so indirectly. Seeing Bindy cooking in the kitchen he might say instead to Leonida in some vague way, *Deine Tochter kocht wieder*, "Your daughter is baking again," strangely removing Bindy's presence from the very action she stood creating just feet from her parents.

Leonida would counter with the fact that Bindy was depleting her baking supplies.

Yet even when he disappeared for hours after work, her father had never returned home drunk, nor had he ever been abusive. As a result, Leonida spent her life compensating for being shortchanged in her marriage, an unhealthy imagining of an artificial balance that sustained her. At times she still allowed herself to recall with romantic fondness the dashing young soldier who had asked her when she was only seventeen years old to marry him, years before her emigration to the States with Bindy's father, but his letter from North Africa six months later admitting to his impending fatherhood had devastated her adolescent dreams. Even as a long-married woman she sometimes saw him in the neighborhood, or at least someone just like him, returned from the faraway continent, still smart in his German uniform, stopping people on the street in his desperate effort to find her in America.

It wasn't just her encounter with Death's entrance into the apartment the night Papa died. Leonida was sure. She knew. She had the sight.

She had once sent Bindy off on a church outing up the Hudson River. Without any parental admonitions to slow her, Bindy had run amok as a wild child, thoroughly enjoying her freedom in the woods, until she had tripped and fallen, spraining her ankle. On the ship back to the 125th Street dock Bindy anxiously sought out the medic onboard. He had wrapped her tender limb in an ace bandage with efficiency, ending with a wan smile. He did his best to make such children feel welcome, but she had been yet one in a long line of faceless children whose worn socks he had tugged back onto an injured foot. He suggested somewhat warmly that she roll up her pant leg to avoid the unforgiving jean material further inciting the ankle's inflammation. Yet, contrary to his advice, she had covered the evidence of her recklessness, a hedge against her mother's keen eye.

She had hardly come through the apartment door when she heard her mother demand from the living room, "Around two o'clock I thought of you so strongly. Let me see what you did to yourself."

And there you had it, thought Bindy. Mom *knew*.

Ich kann es besser. Leonida could always do it better. Bindy had wondered many times why she had not measured up to her mother's expectations, but perhaps it was her mother herself who had not reached her own expectations—an indifferent husband, a static life restraining her active intellectual drive, and a daughter who neither fit nor listened.

Bindy had already grown to an embarrassingly awkward five feet ten inches by the time she was eleven, leaving her rail thin. In addition, the growth spurt had made her clumsy, an annoying quirk Leonida continually mitigated in the presence of other mothers in an evasive effort to draw attention to her own exacting parenting skills instead. She spoke to the women in an imperfect English: "Only by me does she get along." The women praised her *Edelkeit*.

Even years later Bindy could hear the back door to the house slamming—the finalty of it. Clearly, Leonida had wanted her exit to be experienced by more than just herself that last time. She was to be finally recognized. "You fail to show the proper daughterly affection for your parents," Leonida would constantly remind her in the tenement's kitchen. As a child Bindy dreamed *If only I could do everything right for just one day*.

When Bindy announced at nineteen that she would be married, Leonida's response had been "Go and do whatever you want." She could not see that her own daughter had been urging her mother to do the same for years: "If you're so unhappy with Papa, and it's so good over there in the old country as you say, go back. Live with Tante Leah." But Leonida had fears she could not articulate. *Ich weiss mir immer zu helfen.* "I always know how to help myself," she professed. Bindy imagined being left alone with her silent father, a prospect strangely inviting given the lack of a need to justify her American self.

Bindy had never wanted Leonida to come live with her, but in the end she did. "If I hadn't come to help you then you wouldn't have been able to finish college," Leonida confirmed concerning Bindy's college degree, finally acquired at thirty-nine, her only mustered form of congratulation at graduation. Leonida already knew her daughter could not have succeeded without her, viewing her presence in her daughter's house as gift enough.

"Mom, you're absolutely crazy." As an adult Bindy had finally learned to speak with Leonida's lack of reserve, at least when her children were safely occupied in other corners of the house.

Du weist gar nichts, mein Kind. "You know nothing, my child."

Even nearing fifty the common implication stung Bindy.

The last night Leonida stayed in Bindy's house the two had suffered through a terse conversation before dinner. Bindy had wanted to send Leonida to a rest home, just for a month. It was Bindy herself who needed the rest. Plus, there was a German man there, Bindy offered. Perhaps they could talk.

Leonida seethed. "So if I don't behave myself you will throw me out?"

The next morning Bindy had found Leonida's uneaten dinner and untouched glass of champagne, the bubbles now inactive, still on the floor in front of the closed door to her room. Bindy knocked. It was Sunday and time to get ready for church.

Just hours earlier while lying in a warm bed with her husband, the slamming of the back door to the house had startled Bindy awake. Leonida had left, though at the time her daughter could not know her mother's lifeless body lay cold in the downstairs bedroom she had occupied for the past two years. Her mother had willed herself to die that night, one last attempt to sting, but Bindy felt no guilt.

Over the years Bindy's daughters would periodically dream of their grandmother. However, they said that when she tapped on their bedroom doors she was sure to do so gently, entering their dreams without a sound, after which she closed the door of her contact, leaving only the kindness of sleep.

Bindy's dreams were not the same. Once, years after Leonida's death, Bindy had a singular dream. Her mother and Tante Leah were leaning out of the clouds of Heaven: *Wir haben auf dich gewartet aber du bißt nicht gekommen.* The two had been waiting for Bindy but she had not appeared. She had been wanted. But mostly Leonida clouded Bindy's nights by slamming the door over and over, unable to articulate the pain of having to depend on her daughter for so long.

You could have told me so many things a hundred years ago, Mom.

Tochter, in dreams there are a thousand years.

ACKNOWLEDGMENTS

Thanks to Tamara Grayson and Bill Bullock who maintained such faith for many years as I stumbled along, but especially to Sharon Mitchell who was my inspiration for so much and without whom "Vanilla Tuna" would not have come alive one afternoon as a performance of living literature.

Thanks to my parents, Ernie and Nori Schillinger, who gracefully stopped asking about my writing in order to let it happen.

Thanks to all my students, past and present, friends, and extended family whose lives have converged with mine to give me the material of life.

Thanks to Alan Wright and Matt Ankerson for their risks.

And thanks most to Ken who used to let me monopolize our one computer and who, during the process, always seems to say the single thing that turns a story around.

ABOUT THE AUTHOR

Lisa Muir lives at the top of a mountain in Boone, North Carolina, and teaches English at the bottom of the mountain. She holds a Ph.D. in English (American and Ethnic Literature) from West Virginia University and happily lives with her husband Ken, a sociologist.

67 Press is a literary publishing collective founded to give fringe authors a vehicle to be heard. Our goal is finding talented people on the edge of society with something to say, but who don't fit into a neat little box for mainstream publishers. We find talent and help that talent work within their vision to create a finished product. We do all the things that other publishers do, but we do it with the author in mind, not the bottom line or focus groups. We would never tell an author a book doesn't fit into a specific genre, it's too audacious, or "We just don't think it will sell." We believe great stories and great writing transcend subject matter and audience.

If we sound like a publisher you want to work with, please contact us. We'd love to hear from you:

http://67press.com/contact-67-press/